FIVE MOULDY BINS

Five Mouldy Bins

Byron James-Adams

Five Mouldy Bins
Copyright @ 2024 James Byron Books
www.jamesbyronbooks.com

This story is fictitious. Some long-standing institutions, agencies, and public offices do exist.
The characters and situations involved are wholly imaginary, and resemblance to natural persons, living or dead, or actual events is truly coincidental.

Again thanks to my beta readers: Vic, Mel, Lil & M.D.M.
Cover Art: Canva by author.
Internal Book Design: Ingram Sparks.

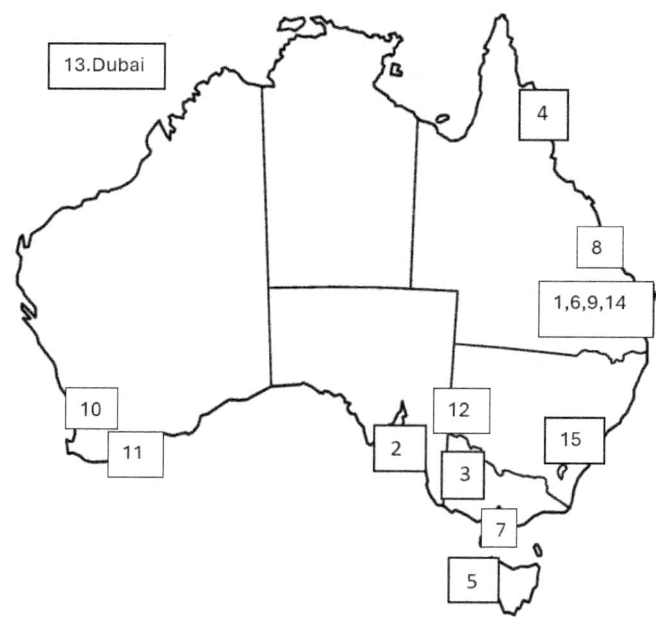

1. Brisbane (Book 1) – One Tricked Phoney
2. Adelaide (Book 1)
3. Pinnaroo (Book 1)
4. Port Douglas (Book 2) – Two Hurtled Gloves
5. Corrina (Book 2)
6. Brisbane (Book 2)
7. Melbourne (Book 3) – Three French Bens
8. Rockhampton (Book 3)
9. Brisbane (Book 3)
10. Busselton (Book 4) – Four Brooding Birds
11. Margaret River (Book 4)
12. Boolcoomatta Reserve (Book 4)
13. Dubai (Book 5) – Five Mouldy Bins
14. Brisbane (Book 5)
15. Sydney (Book 5)

1

It was mid-July, around noon, and another cloudless winter's day in Brisbane, South East Queensland. Rosemary Palmer was standing in a cardboard box, dressed as a Christmas tree adorned with festive decorations. The box was waist-high, full of baubles and her arms were held out at ninety degrees dripping with red and green tinsel.

A small crowd of old timers were gathered around, taking turns throwing the tinsel over her head, and an elderly gentleman shuffled forward with a big grin and a sprig of mistletoe in his hand. Rose looked at him and wondered how she would get out of kissing him - after all, it was the tradition.

'Hello Mr Cook, how is your wife these days? Is she here somewhere? Is that why you have the mistletoe?'

The man stopped mid-stride, looked at his hand, then at Rose. 'This isn't mistletoe, young lady. It's my lunch. I'm a vegan you know.' He shuffled off and began munching on the festive sprig.

An announcement then interrupted the Christmas chaos: 'Welcome to The Hamilton Village Retirement Centre. It's Christmas in July, Ladies and Gentlemen, boys and girls. Santa will be arriving within the hour.'

A toddler was now standing in front of Rose, and she tried her best not to stare down at the boy, but eventually conceded to his cheeky charm. 'If you like I can give you some of this tinsel, and you can pretend you are a Christmas tree, too.'

The boy looked at her and squirmed a little. 'My dad told me not to talk to strangers, and you look very strange dressed as a tree, but the man there told me to ask you something.'

Rose looked over at her friend and scam-busting business associate, Nic Thorn. He was dressed as an elf and gave her a silly grin. Rose looked back down at the boy. 'Sure, what is that little man?'

'How does Father Christmas get all around the world in one night?'

As Rose stammered for the response, one of the adults had recognised the signs of someone in distress from a young child's awkward and inevitable Christmas question. A woman approached Rose, took the boy's hand and began to lead him away. 'I hope my grandson wasn't bothering you, Miss

Tree. He tends to be fascinated by anything to do with Christmas.'

Rose's BFF, Sandy Fraser walked up. 'You look like you need a break. Do you want me to take over for a while? I won't be much good as a tree though, as I'm a blonde and can't wear red and green to-gether.'

Rose sighed. 'Can you help me anyway?'

'Sorry, I need to practice playing the Christmas carols on the piano.'

'Very funny, Sandy. Please grab someone and help me out of this stupid box.'

Rose started to move her legs and found she was stuck fast. 'I'm stuck. I knew it wasn't a good idea to allow Nic to bounce the children on the baubles in the box as it's compressed them down.'

Rose wriggled and jiggled from side to side, and the box started moving when suddenly there was an explosion of bright-coloured balls as the sides had given way. The box and Rose toppled onto the floor sending the balls and tinsel everywhere. A couple of baubles rolled toward Nic, and he picked two of them up to start juggling. Rose rolled onto her back still trying to get up.

'Damn you, Nic. Stop showing off, and help me.'

'You'll be fine, and besides, I'm on a roll here. I've got two baubles in the air.'

Sandy assisted Rose to her feet 'How about you add another one, and make it challenging.'

Nic bent down to grab another bauble whilst keeping the other two in the air, one-handed and now had three in the air.

Rose approached Nic. 'Show off,' then plucked one from the air during his juggle, grabbed a couple of candy canes and started herself. Rose had three baubles and two candy canes in her arc.

Nic stopped and watched. 'That's impressive. I didn't know you had such hidden talents and didn't read that on your Vita Brevis dating app. Just how many can you go?'

'There are some secrets best left alone, and juggling is one of them. Eleven is the most anyone can do, and my best is four. I once got caught juggling a couple of my father's paperweights and dropped one onto his foot. It mashed his big toe. I was twenty-five at the time.'

Rose kept juggling, and Sandy piped up. 'So we have a juggle off, ladies and gentlemen, Christmas style. Anyone want to lay some money down on my Miss Tree against Mr Juggle?'

Nic collected the balls from Rose's arc in mid-flight. 'Sorry to disappoint I've got to go. There's something about an impending appearance of a jolly fellow in a big red suit.'

Sandy laughed as they watched him leave. 'I bet that wasn't on his Vita Brevis dating app, that Nic Thorn plays Saint Nick.'

About an hour later, most of the elderly patrons had been corralled outside and joined with the crowd of children eagerly awaiting the arrival of Father Christmas.

A small, motorised float arrived, and a single line of two reindeer was pulling it. The jolly red man had pride of place in the sleigh, but the reindeer were four men dressed in faux deer outfits. The suits were poorly designed and poorly patched together. One man had the head, and the other was bent down behind, harbouring the rear.

The children squealed with delight, and some of the adults, too.

Rose leaned into Sandy. 'So, do you think the jolly red man is Nic?'

'He could be. It looks like he stacked on about fifty kilograms in half an hour, but he does have access to various latex suits for a disguise.'

Rose shook her head. 'Nope, I reckon he's one of the reindeer, probably the one with the blinking red nose. Rudolf is in the house.'

The sleigh pulled to a stop at the front of the retirement centre, and Santa stood up with welcoming arms but quickly sat down again as the sleigh lurched forward as the brake must not have been appropriately set. The drive shaft made its point with the closest reindeer and jabbed it in the rump.

The reindeer/man raised his head quickly, instantly severing the poorly sewn joint between the head and the rear. 'Ow, that hurt', and he looked back at Santa. 'You stupid oaf, I told you to put the brake on as soon as we stopped.'

His head was now out of the costume, and some children screamed in horror. Some of the adults, too.

'Well, that's definitely not Nic.' Rose quickly added.

The man looked around, realised he'd scared the gathered crowd, stepped out of the costume, left the crumpled torso and two feet in a pile, and ran off. Some of the younger children now saw that the reindeer, or what was left of it, only had half a body and began to wail.

Santa quickly tried to take control of the situation. 'Ho, Ho, Ho everybody. Santa is here, and I will take good care of my Blitzen. Don't worry.'

Rose stifled a laugh. 'I don't think that Santa is Nic either. His voice isn't that deep.' Sandy nodded. 'I suppose you're right, so he must be Rudolf. Well, one half of Rudolf, who knows noses, knows Rose.'

Meanwhile, the other half of Blitzen realised his rear was missing and removed the costume head. This caused more children to wail, so he quickly put the head back on and galloped to placate the children. He then started neighing like a horse and shaking his head from side to side.

It wasn't working.

One of the residents then approached Rose and Sandy. 'I told them this would be a disaster. We should have used elves instead. They're so much easier to control. I have some living in my room.' Sandy looked at her. 'Real elves?'

'Yes, they're very naughty. They hide my car keys and eat all my food too. Sometimes they even change the channels on the TV.'

'Do they have special names? What do they look like?'

The woman cackled and walked away. 'Oh no, they're invisible.' Rose and Sandy watched as she picked phantom fairy dust from the air.

The duo decided to approach Rudolf, and Sandy started stroking the side of the reindeer's head. 'Great nose, by the way. Does it do Morse Code?'

The red rose started blinking a lot more. 'Is that you in there, Nic?'

Rudolf leaned into her shoulder and started rolling his head. Rose looked at the head rubbing. 'I don't think that's Nic in there either. He doesn't do PDAs.'

'Oh, you're right. No Public Displays of Attention from our Nic.' Sandy stopped the caressing and tried to move away, but the reindeer kept nuzzling her.

Meantime, Santa stepped down from the sleigh and entered the retirement centre, pulling sweets from his red sack and handing them out. Rudolf released himself from the halter and was now trailing along behind, so Rose went up and slapped him hard on the rump. There was no reaction.

The crowd moved back inside, and Santa sat in an oversized chair in the middle of the recreation room. 'Ho, Ho, Ho, everybody. Santa is here. I will take care of my Blitzen. Don't worry.'

Rose moved closer to Rudolf. 'Where did you find *this* Santa? He's a bit limited with the Christmas jargon.' Rudolf shook his head from side to side and moved over the stand beside the large, jolly red man.

Another resident walked up to Sandy. 'You know, young lady, I look forward to singing the carols. I'm in fine voice and everything. They told me you are playing the piano.'

Sandy smiled. 'Err, sure. I'm, um, yep, I'll be doing that. We have to wait for Santa to leave, though.' He looked at her. 'I'm sorry if I come across as grumpy sometimes. The IRS is giving me much grief now, you know.'

Sandy nodded. 'That's OK, as we must deal with death and taxes. They say it's the things that catch up with all of us in the end.'

The man walked off and broke into his version of White Christmas. He didn't know the words, the tune, or that he was severely off-key.

Rose was still determined to get Rudolf/Nic to reveal himself but eventually gave up as too many children were clambering around Santa trying to sit on his lap, so they moved back. Rose leaned into Sandy. 'What did old Mr Lambert say to you?'

'We talked about death and taxes. You know, the IRS, that sort of thing.'

'The IRS is the American Tax system – Internal Revenue Service. I don't think he's an American.'

'I've no idea. What else would it be then?'

'Hold on, I'll check with one of the nurses.' Rose moved over to the Head Nurse and returned after a quick conversation. 'It's not the IRS that he's afraid of, it's the IBS.'

'What's IBS, Rose?'

'Irritable Bowel Syndrome.'

They decided they'd had enough of waiting for Nic to reveal that he was one part of Rudolf, so they went up to the reindeer again. Rose clamped her arm around the head, Sandy grabbed the rear, and they pushed the beast towards the kitchen and it showed little resistance.

Sandy whispered, 'Come on, Nic, are you the head or the rear?'

They reached the kitchen, swung the door open, stepped through, and were shocked at what they saw as Nic was standing at the sink doing the dishes. He grinned. 'I guess you've got some explaining to do.'

The head and tail of the reindeer separated revealing two well-known State politicians: the Minister for Aged Care and his Chief of Staff. The two men sloughed the costumes and placed them on the kitchen bench. The younger one was gingerly rubbing his backside.

Nic grinned. 'Say hello to the Honourable Mr Paul Roberts and his EA, Phillip Robertson. Paul is the Head of the Queensland Department of Health, and together represent the backbone of Aged Care. Gentlemen, please let me introduce my associates, Miss Sandy Fraser and Miss Rose Palmer.' The two men shook hands with them, said nothing, and left the kitchen.

Rose sighed. 'I should have known it wasn't you under there, Nic. You never quit whilst you're a head, nor tend to make an ass of yourself in public.'

'Thanks, I think.' Nic then picked up the head of the costume, and one plastic eye fell off. 'Rose, you still have 'no-eye deer' about me, do you?'

'Laugh it up, you Saint Nick wannabe.'

2

Rose and Sandy moved towards Nic softly punching his shoulders and Rose added. 'What are we here to investigate? Or were you 'voluntold' to attend to this soirée? Does it have something to do with your Community Service debt for forgetting to comply with a Santa clause?'

Nic shrugged and handed them each a tea towel. 'Here, start wiping. Let's finish the dishes, then head back to my place to run over the gist of the investigation.'

Sandy piped up. 'What about singing the carols? I'm supposed to be playing the piano. I am in demand, you know, Elton John told me so a minute ago.'

Rose nodded 'When did you meet Elton? I didn't know he was here today.'

'Yes, he's the big guy with the big wig and the big bright green glasses. He told me his name was Elton and proceeded to belt out a song. I think it was Candle in the Wind. He said I might not recognise it as he didn't know the words or the tune.'

Nic shook his head. 'Sorry Sandy, but we have other things to do. Besides, pushing the 'on' button on a Casio keyboard isn't really playing it, but then Karaoke is not really singing, is it?'

Sandy nodded. 'I guess not. We caught the ferry around from the West End, so do you have your car, or can we grab a sleigh ride back with Santa? He must be heading off to the city soon as Santa Land must be missing him.'

Nic shook his head. 'Don't worry, we've got a ride. It is a ten-seater Retirement Centre minibus. I'll get their driver to run us home.'

The group completed their kitchen duties and went outside, where the bus was waiting. The driver stepped out to greet them: it was Rose's ex-husband's wife, Dimond. Her husband, Michael, had married Rose about ten years ago. The marriage was a sham, lasted three long days, and had to do with a business deal that Rose's father was trying to put together. The deal fell over and so did the marriage. Rose is yet to forgive her parents.

Dimond was standing with her hands on her hips. 'Hi, you three, before you say anything, yes, I am the driver, and before you say anything else, it is part of my community service. And before you say anything more, I got drunk one night after

Michael threatened to leave. He told me that I was celebrating too much, so he called the police.'

The trio looked at her, but Rose spoke first. 'How does that earn you community service?'

'I sort of, well, um.....I'm not that good with cars. I attacked Michaels's car with an axe, shaving cream, and a hedge trimmer. It was going great until he reminded me he had lent *our* car to his Boss. Isn't funny how all Accountant's cars look the same, but then again, so do most Accountants.'

Rose shook her head. 'So, they pressed charges?'

'Yes, as I pleaded guilty they wrote off the damages as a business expense. I've got a month or two of driving old people around, but at least it gives me the heads up on when beds come available in the retirement village.'

'Not for yourself, surely? You're not even thirty.'

'No, it's for my grandparents. They are looking to move down from Bundaberg, and this retirement centre is in the suburb where I've been looking for a new home. I want to move from Morningside to this side of the Brisbane River. The cross-river ferry is getting too expensive these days. Michael tells me we can't claim the ferry ticket cost any longer. Apparently, it's not a tax deduction to take your children to school by ferry. Who knew?'

They stepped onto the bus, headed towards Southbank and Dimond announced over the onboard intercom: 'Thank you for travelling in the Hamilton Retirement Centre Fun Bus. It's great having you young'uns aboard as I don't have to explain where I'm going or if we'll be back in time to take your medication.'

Nic directed her to stop at the turnout of his apartment complex, and Dimond was a little disappointed as she wasn't invited to come up with them. 'I have seen inside your apartment. The maintenance guy has a key that lets you in. I convinced him I needed to drop a bouquet inside on Valentine's Day.'

'Thanks, but can you make them Lisianthus next time? That way, I can pass them on to Rose instead of giving them to old Mrs Davis in Apartment 11. She nearly had a heart attack when she found out I'd left them for her in the foyer.'

Dimond continued. 'Will do, and just so you know, Michael is quite jealous of how much time we spent together.'

Rose piped up. 'Just what have you told Michael? Nic doesn't spend any time with you.'

'No, but it keeps him thinking. Besides, since the day Nic told him to stop harassing you, he's a changed man.' They looked at her.

'You know, I sometimes catch him staring at your wedding pictures, Rose. You know it's been over ten years, but Michael still hasn't forgiven himself for walking out on you at the airport. You were supposed to be going on your honeymoon and everything.' Rose shook her head. 'I think I'm going to be sick. He'd promised me that all the photos were destroyed.'

Dimond sighed. 'Well, don't be sick in here. I've only cleaned up the mess from the day I took the retirement crowd to the Caravan and Camping Show. It all went sideways when they opened the bags of fairy floss and started chugging on the free sample bottles of sherry.'

They exited the bus, making their way past Dimond sitting in the driver's seat, and she held out a black and silver box. 'Always remember to touch on and touch off when completing your journey.'

Rose took the box from her. 'This is a Sony Walkman Cassette player. I haven't seen one of these for years. What scam are you pulling here, Dimond?'

'Well, the usual passengers don't know what it is. So I get them to hold their hands over it and I say '*bing*', then take five dollars from them.'

Sandy looked at her. 'I assume the money goes back to the retirement village?'

'No way, it covers my time as a bus driver. Michael says it provides spending money for me and my children, Skye, and Lucy.'

'That's dishonest, Dimond.'

'It probably is, but it's not a lie if you believe it.'

Rose and Sandy looked at Nic. 'Hey, that's not one of my idioms. I think it's a George quote from that Seinfeld TV show.'

They finally made their way from the bus and Dimond also stepped out. Rose moved towards her. 'Can I ask you a serious question, Dimond?'

'Sure, but I hope it's not about Michael.'

Rose shook her head in disbelief. 'No, it's not. Why did you name your children Skye and Lucy? You do know about The Beatles' song 'Lucy in the Sky with Diamonds?''

'Yes, I do. I liked the song, and Michael said the naming thing was entirely my choice. He could only come up with boy names, like Michael the Second or Michael Junior, so he refused to participate. He wasn't even there when I, you know, went into the hospital. He said he was busy, and I found out later that he was having a haircut. Both times.'

As they approached the apartment foyer, Rose turned around, stepped back into the mini-bus, and removed the Walkman. They waved Dimond off but noticed that she had picked up a blue Tupperware lunch box and put it in place of the Walkman.

The group then took the elevator up to Nic's apartment, and he hesitated. 'I've made some changes since you were here last. The biggest one is that I have a housekeeper, and her name is Ivy.' They were now at the apartment door, and Rose noticed there was no longer a key lock. It was just a glass pin-pad panel. Nic faced the door. 'Hello Ivy, I'm home. Unlock, please.'

There was a click, and the door swung open, but no one was there. 'Thanks, Ivy.'

Rose and Sandy stepped in and the door closed behind them. Rose looked around the room. 'What's the trick, Nic? Where is Ivy?'

'Oh, sorry, it's I.V.E - Integrated Voice Evolution. Chewy is up from Melbourne and has been wiring it all up and we are trialling it in my apartment.'

Rose smiled. 'So you managed to get him out of his geeky computer basement to set up a geeky apartment. What happened to all the dragons in his dungeon? Are they here up on holiday too?'

'No, they are too big to put in the overhead luggage. Did you know they had to ban it in the United States as too many dragons were being flushed down the toilets?'

A man moved out of one of the apartment rooms. Rose and Sandy had met Chewy in Melbourne during one of their other investigations. He was Nic's computer go-to guy. The man was dressed in three-quarter length pants, a high-vis shirt, Blundstone work boots and had headphones on. His eyes were closed and he was oblivious to their presence. He also appeared to be counting down on his fingers and almost ran directly into the kitchen bench, then stopped, stepped to his right, and kept walking towards the front door.

Finally, he opened his eyes. 'Hey, mate. We're good to go here. Ivy is locked and loaded. All the doors, windows, and drawers will lock when you are not here.'

He nodded to Rose and Sandy. 'This place gets shut down like a drum as soon as you leave. Ivy will let you know if anyone is at the front door, or if they manage to get in, exactly where they go.'

Rose nodded. 'What happens if there is a power loss?'

'It's got a solar battery backup.'

Rose added. 'What happens if Nic wants someone else to come in here, and he's off with his wizards and fairies somewhere?'

'We can work with that, too. Ivy can recognise your voices and store them. It will allow you access to the apartment, but only areas that Nic has authorised. So you can't get into his bedroom or meet the troll that lives under his bed without his permission.'

'What if we want to use the...um...you know...the facilities?'

'We can set that up too, but only selected bathrooms.'

'What if...?'

Nic looked at her. 'Boy, you ask a lot of questions. Let's get the dinner on and look into the

Aged Care thing we've been asked to look into.' Rose looked at Nic. 'What Ivy doesn't cook as well? It's all futuristic, George Jenson TV stuff, but Ivy sounds like an overly ambitious version of the Google appliances already available.'

Chewy grinned. 'Ah, it's more than that. This one is mobile and interfaces with Android and iPhones. It's linked to Nic's watch and an app on the phone. It's better than an appliance that sits on your dining table and squawks whenever you talk to it. Let's open a bottle of wine and get this party started.'

Nic held out his arm and showed them his watch. It was just a black square face on his forearm. 'I've got a small magnetic microchip embedded in my skin, which holds it in place, so no need for a band. There's also an earpiece behind my ear.' He pulled back his ear and showed them. 'I can make and take calls, and it helps me with all the other phoney stuff that I do too.'

Sandy nodded. 'Cool. When do we get one?'

Nic grinned. 'It's a one-of-a-kind, like me.'

They were seated around the dining table when Nic's watch rang, so he moved away to take the call and sat on the couch. 'Yes, it's been a very long time, Xanthe. How are you doing? Wow, he's finally put a ring on your finger; it's about time.' There was a lot of nod and smiling, and then he hung up. He said nothing to the others, sat momentarily, stood, sat back at the table, and continued eating.

Rose looked at him. 'Spill it, Nic. The last time you mentioned someone called Xanthe was when you told us about an Ice Hockey queen trying out for the Olympics. You said she'd broken both legs and it was your fault, and she went into hospital but never came out.'

'Yep, that's all true. Xanthe became a Doctor and stayed in there, but that's not why she rang. The engagement ring was supposed to be worth about fifty thousand dollars, but when she had it valued for insurance purposes, the report said it was worth less than three.'

Rose nodded. 'So, she got scammed. Besides that, how come she still had your number? I deleted Michael's the day after I left him.'

'I thought you said it was the day you married him?'

'Actually, you're right.'

Nic continued. 'Her fiancé, the wonderful Dr Gabriel Goodenough, won the ring on a television game show. He took the ring instead of the cash and proposed to Xanthe during the show's taping.'

Rose took over again. 'Why did she say yes? A proposal is supposed to be private and subtle, and between two people in love, not some staged circus performance served with popcorn.'

'Duly noted. Anyhow, they want me to find out where the discrepancy originated, whether from the show, the jeweller, the supplier or elsewhere. Gabriel is not too happy about it. All he knows is that the diamond came from Africa.'

Sandy suddenly broke into a laugh. 'His surname is Goodenough. She left the wonderful Nic Thorn and is getting married to someone called 'Goodenough?''

Nic nodded. 'We split up over ten years ago, but perhaps she's never found Mister Right and settled for the next best thing that just might be good enough.'

Chewy looked at Nic. 'So, what do you have in mind?'

Nic took a breath. 'I'm not sure if we should get involved, but sometimes it's good to do something for nothing, right?'

Rose looked at him. 'Why the second thoughts? Is the gilt coming off your shining armour?'

Nic stood up and struck the classic 'Superman' pose, then brushed at the sleeves of his shirt. 'I don't think so, but I've heard that you can't always be a hero to everyone.'

'Is that from a comic book hero?'

'Nope, it's from Thorn, Nic Thorn.'

'Good grief. What's the issue, then? Money? Time? A long lost unrequited love?'

'No, to all of those, Rose.' Nic then looked over to Chewy. 'How long will it take to assemble a pilot for an online quiz show? We'll put up a prize for a round trip to South Africa, which should get us there without raising suspicion. Let's run it from my warehouse at Bowen Hills. The show will be a super quick answering game. We'll need a name for the show, too. Any ideas?'

Rose piped up. 'How about Brain Haq? As in Body Hack, like that show on TV with that advertising guy that only ever wears t-shirts.'

'Great idea.' This came from Chewy, then he added. 'Do we have a budget?'

'K.I.S.S, Chewy. Keep It Simple and Stupid. We don't need much spent on it.'

Rose added. 'How can you guarantee that you will win?'

'Boy Rose, you're full of good questions today. It's my show, my rules, and my game.'

Rose nodded. 'Isn't that the case with everything you do?'

Nic grinned. 'You're right, but I can live with that.'

Sandy leaned back and stretched. 'So what happens to the old people scam we are supposed to be looking into then? We can't wait too long, as we might lose some witnesses.'

'Today was just a meet and greet. I'll leave Chewy to do some data mining using his computer stuff in Melbourne. The story is that someone near the top of the Aged Care system is involved. The Queensland State opposition team has brought me in as they estimate millions are unaccounted for in the Aged Care budget. It has to be dealt with all very quietly and all very carefully.'

Sandy nodded. 'Don't the political party boys always say that about each other and eventually leak something to the press? Fake news and all that?'

Nic smiled. 'There might be actual evidence, so that's why we've been brought in. To move a bit of sand around, hopefully, it doesn't reveal the local cat has been using it as a litter tray.'

'So?'

'Well, I was going to talk to Paul Roberts and Phillip Robertson, the two guys playing Rudolf, but you guys scared them off with a serious case of reindeer harassment. I won't be surprised if I get a call from Santa, and you two will not be on his nice list this year.'

Sandy shook her head, and Rose responded. 'Damn, you, Saint Nic.'

They finished the meal, and Rose and Sandy caught a ferry to their home at West End. Their Maine Coon cat, Dog, was pleased to see they had arrived as he welcomed them home with a loud meow. He was toying with a foam float ball attached to a two-metre-thick marine rope and would have dragged it up from the nearby Brisbane riverbank.

Rose pointed it out to Sandy. 'Big rope.'

Sandy nodded. 'Big cat.'

3

A week later, they were at Nic's warehouse in Bowen Hills watching the pilot's progress. A stage was arranged with lecterns for four groups of three people. A large neon sign blinked above the area. It read: '*Welcome to Brain Haq.*'

Chewy was setting up cameras, the stagehands were making final touches to the lighting, and the sound technicians were checking the acoustics. A piano had been brought in, so Nic guided Sandy and Rose to take a seat. 'OK, guys, your job is to develop a song for the opening credits.'

They looked at him, Rose sat down on the right-hand side, and Sandy brought up another chair to sit on the left. Rose took a breath. 'What do you want us to do, hammer down on the keys until we find something that resembles a tune?'

'Yep, that's about it. Chewy has hooked it up to a computer, so as long as you keep to some consistency, it will put something together.'

After a couple of minutes, they came up with a little melody, and then Nic hit the record button on the laptop and they sat back to wait for the magic to happen. The computer added a drum line, a subtle guitar sound, and a bit of brass, and then it stopped. Nic hit playback, and they had their opening tune for the rolling credits.

Rose had been bopping along to the beat. 'Can we name the song Nic?'

'Sure.'

'Let's call it 'The Rose.''

'It's been done before...Rose'

'How about 'The Piano Man?''

Nic shook his head. 'Now, that was a great Billy Joel song. How about I come up with the song title?'

'Sure, but you'll take the credit and steal all the royalties.'

He laughed. 'OK, let's call it 'The Brain Haq Theme Song.''

Sandy stood up. 'Wow, now that took a lot of thought.' Chewy approached them and listened to the playback. 'That's a catchy beat if you take out the piano part.'

The trio wandered around the set, then sat at a table covered in leads, camera cases and computers. Sandy looked at the cameras, then at Nic. 'Surely we won't be filmed. I thought you wanted us to keep a quiet, non-existent social profile. Nic

'The Batman' will finally be unmasked if it turns up on the internet.'

'It's all good, Sandy. We are using avatars.'

Rose nodded. 'The pretty, blue, tall, stretchy men from that pretty blue film?' They looked at Rose. 'Yep, I saw that one. I do go to the movies sometimes. I like James Cameron films, but the one with the ship going down was disappointing. I thought he could have changed the ending.'

'It was a true story, the sinking of the Titanic.'

'Yes, I know, but in the recent Leo DeCap and Brad Pitt movie, the one with Charlie Manson, they changed the ending, and Sharon Tate didn't get murdered.'

Nic nodded. 'He also did the Terminator movies. The one with big Arnie.'

'I haven't seen those, but wasn't he the Governor of California too?'

Nic smiled. 'You know your Hollywood stuff. You'll do great in the quiz show.'

Rose grinned. 'Thanks, but I never agreed to be a part of your disaster movie.'

Nic continued. 'Well, there are three seats, and Chewy will be directing the show. I'll need you two up on stage with me to beat the other 'know-it-all's on the other teams.'

'I thought you said the show would be rigged, and you'll win anyway?'

'Yep, I did say that.'

'So why do you need Sandy and me? You could get anyone to sit with you and change them into avatars. I can call Michael and Dimond. I'm sure he'd love to show you how smart he is.'

'You said you don't have his number.'

'Nope, but you do.'

'No, I don't.'

'Well, we know where Dimond is. I'm sure she could tear herself away from bus driving duties for a few hours.'

Nic shook his head. 'Nope, that won't work either, sorry. I couldn't trust them; besides, I would have to bring them into our world of solving scams and frauds, and from what I know about Michael, he's already ventured into the dark side.'

Sandy laughed, 'Good segue. That's another of James Cameron's great films.'

Rose looked at them. 'I know that name, isn't he's from Star Wars. The robot thingy with the gold suit.' Chewy came up, looked at her, and started barking like Chewbacca. 'Darth Vader was Luke's father, and C3PO was the gold droid robot. You still haven't seen the films yet, have you?'

'Nope. I missed the first one in seventy-seven as that was well before I was born, so thought I leave it until they're all finished or may binge-watch them once Nic has left our lives.'

Nic nodded. 'Now that's something to look forward to.'

Rose grinned. 'Which one? You leaving us or binge-watching the films?'

Nic added. 'You chose.'

'Damn you, Nic. Hey, I just realised something, if the cheap diamond scam originated in Africa, and we win the trip to Africa for being the 'Brain Haq' champions, doesn't that mean you are finally taking Sandy and me overseas?'

Nic sighed. 'I thought you'd missed that part.'

Rose grinned. 'Africa it is then. That's a country that neither of us has been yet.'

Nic shook his head. 'It could be, or it might be the United Emirates, or somewhere completely different. It depends on where the evidence takes us, and this time, as it's a favour to a friend, I'll have to monitor the expenses.'

'Great, so if it gets too expensive, you'll have to down-grade our flights to Economy. We don't like flying anything besides Business Class, you know that.'

'Well, you could pay for your tickets.'

'Damn you again, Nic.'

Chewy then waved to one of his cohorts, and a young woman walked over. She introduced herself as 'Dee-Dee' and was holding a laptop, then placed it on the table before her. 'Dee-Dee is doing the avatars. You are only limited by your imagination. So whatever you want to be, we can set it up.'

Dee-Dee took over. 'Nic has chosen to be a matronly professor, a woman of about sixty with blue rinse hair and bifocals. Any ideas from you two?'

Rose shook her head. 'Are our voices disguised as well?'

'Yes, they will be, along with everything else.'

'OK. I want to be a Brad Pitt look-a-like, with the voice of Sean Connery.'

Dee-Dee tapped a few buttons and then spun the computer around.

'That was quick.'

Dee-Dee nodded. 'Well, Nic had mentioned some names to me, so I had a template ready. It was a toss-up between Brad Pitt and Pierce Brosnan. I went with Brad. Are you OK with that?'

'Yes, but can I be the younger version of him from Thelma and Louise film?'

Dee-Dee nodded. 'Sure.'

Sandy leaned in. 'I would like to be tall, a redhead, with a killer smile....'

Dee-Dee clicked a few buttons and spun the screen around. Jessica Rabbit from the 1988 film 'Who Framed Roger Rabbit' appeared.

'Not quite Dee-Dee. I can't do the Kathleen Turner sultry voice to match that cartoon.'

Dee-Dee spun the laptop back around, pressed a few keys and came up with another option. It was an image of the blonde actress from Game Of Thrones. 'Will this do?'

Sandy nodded. 'I often wondered if I could ever be a queen and a dragon at the same time.' Nic smiled. 'Upload and save them, Dee-Dee.'

Dee-Dee nodded, then walked off to talk to the other groups. Rose whispered. 'I thought you didn't use real names in your investigations. It would be easy to track down a Dee-Dee on Facebook.'

'Dee-Dee is not her name. It's her job.'

'What?'

'Yes, Dee-Dee. It stands for 'Data Delivery.''

Rose shook her head. 'Where to from here then? When does the pilot get taped?'

'In about an hour, we'll do a full rehearsal; then the show is filmed at two p.m. tomorrow. The other guys are from 'Rent-A-Crowd' and will play a role. It may get a bit animated as they're working from a loose script, but it will all add to the drama. The questions will appear on a monitor in front of each team, and they will have five seconds to answer. It's multiple choice, A, B, C or D.'

Sandy nodded. 'How will we know the right answer?'

'We don't have a choice as only one answer will appear on our screen. Even if we don't answer it in five seconds, we'll get it correct anyway.'

Rose smiled. 'That's real cheating, isn't it?'

'Yep, my show, my rules. Besides, have you seen the questions? They're hard.'

About an hour later, Chewy called to everyone to take their nominated seats. Most of them did. However, a couple were still sitting at the table with Dee-Dee and he called over to them.

'What's up Dee-Dee? We need them to take their seats now, please.'

Dee-Dee nodded. 'Sorry, they're one short as one of them had to leave. His wife is not well, so he had to go to look after the kids.'

'OK, just throw in a dancing baby as the third avatar with them. They're all over the internet; grab one of the images.'

'Roger that.'

The couple went to their seats, and Chewy sat at the console desk. 'We go live in fifteen seconds.'

Sandy leaned into Nic. 'I thought this was a rehearsal?'

'It could be, but it depends on how it goes. We may still film tomorrow's pilot, then cut and paste the best bits.'

'So, it's not live then?'

'No, but neither are the other TV game shows, so it won't matter. It's all about building drama, selling the anticipation, and booking the advertising space.'

Chewy spoke into his microphone. '5, 4, 3, 2...' and dropped his forefinger and the monitors in front of the desks blinked on. Everyone got to see what their avatars looked like, and the trio of young people sitting two desks over from Nic's group burst out laughing. 'Cut'. Chewy called out. 'What's happened, guys?'

'Sorry, I've got a green shirt on, so it shows that my head is detached from my body.' The young man continued to move his head around, and it appeared on the monitor screen as if it was floating of its own accord. 'OK, change your shirt, but remember I'm looking at your avatar, not the monitor.'

The young man pulled his shirt off and had a t-shirt underneath. It read "Free the Wales", and he raised his hand to get Chewy's attention.

'What's up?'

'Is this too political?' Chewy told the young man to put his hand down, started the countdown again, and the introduction music played. Nic smiled and whispered. 'Good job, guys.'

Another avatar appeared in the monitors before them, and a voice-over came through the sound speakers: It was a caricature of Albert Einstein with the swagger of Elvis Presley. The voice was distinctly British and began introducing the show's concept:

'Ladies and Gentlemen, welcome to Brain Haq. The show where our Teams go up against your teams. It's an entirely interactive Question and Answer show. If you are smart enough and quick enough, you might win the prize, thanks to the team at Flight World. Today's prize is a plane ticket for three people to the destination of your choice, to the value of twenty-five thousand dollars.'

The avatar suddenly started buffering, catching Albert in a half-Elvis wiggle, so Chewy shut it down. 'Sorry guys, I've picked up some interference here. Is someone using a mobile phone or a tablet?' One of the group members sitting next to Nic pointed to a young woman on the other side of him. 'I think she's googling something on her phone.'

The young woman sheepishly owned up. 'I'm sorry, I didn't know who the old dude was, so I googled him. Albert Einstein, wow, and he's also a great dancer for a Brainiac.'

Nic whispered. 'Kids.'

Chewy re-started the show, and the narrative continued. 'There are six rounds of six questions; you can call 'double down', earning you double points on any two questions. Remember, if you get it wrong, you've doubled down on the loss of points too.' Albert continued to dance his way through the topics of questions: 'Ladies and Gentlemen, please start your neurons.'

The first topic was History, and most of the group got the answers within the designated time. The show continued, but halfway through the fourth round, two men started slapping at the different buttons on their pulpits. It was all getting heated and a bit nasty.

Finally, the eldest of the men stood up and threatened to punch the other. Nic looked over and smiled. 'I think they just read their script.' Both men stood up and walked off the stage, leaving the single avatar alone. Nic looked over to Chewy, and he gave the double thumbs up.

It came down to the last round, and Sandy leaned into Nic. 'I thought I knew stuff about stuff, but this stuff is well beyond me.' Sandy leaned forward to Rose for confirmation and saw that Rose had been writing some of the answers down on a small notepad. The show finished up, the music started up again and the groups stood and huddled around each other.

Chewy stood up. 'That's a wrap. Thanks, everyone.'

Nic's group came together at the console, and Chewy was happy with the result. 'I'm not sure if we have to do another pilot tomorrow. I'll send this to my TV guys to see what they think.'

Nic noticed Rose had been taking notes. 'How did you go? The questions are hard, aren't they?'

'I reckon I probably scored about thirty out of the forty.'

Nic took the notepad from her and compared them to the answers. 'Yep, you did well. I didn't know you knew so much stuff about stuff. I'll know where to go next time if I need to know stuff about stuff.'

'Hey, I went to Uni. I read the papers and I used to play Trivial Pursuit. My brother and I lost all the little chips from the game, so we just asked each other the questions. We weren't allowed to watch much TV growing up.'

'Duly noted for the next Pub Quiz night. Are we good here, Chewy?'

'Yes, the two men fighting over the question were sketchy, though. Their avatars were Mr and Mrs Potato-Head. It will be good for TV, but that's about it.'

'OK, can you settle the 'Rent-A-Crowd' invoice? I'll take these two Brainiacs home. It is so damn exhausting being, really, really, good-looking and really, really smart.'

Rose added. 'Speak for yourself, Nic.'

'I was.'

4

It was 8 p.m., a few days later, and Nic was at Sandy's house in West End. Dog was feverishly clawing its way up Nic's trouser leg trying to get to him to sit down. Nic finally complied, and Rose grinned. 'Dog really likes you.'

'I know, whenever I come here, he wants to sit on my lap and purr. He sounds like my Ford Mustang on idle.'

Rose grinned. 'So, Cat-Man, where are we up to with the Aged Care thing? And what's the latest with Brain Haq?'

'Chewy said it went well, so we'll launch the show on a new online-only TV channel next week. It will be slotted between 'Stop The Drain Brain' and 'Make My Head Hurt.''

Sandy added. 'We've already won the show, why the need to put us online?'

'It legitimises the prize, and our ability to be tourists wherever we end up.'

'So, have you worked out where the rabbit hole leads us down to?'

'Well, the good news is that the diamond is not Australian, so, we are going overseas to track down its origin. The bad news is it's either to Russia or Botswana.'

'Why is that bad news?'

'Do either of you speak Russian or Swahili?'

Rose shook her head. 'Nope.'

'I don't either, but I know a couple that do, and that's a worry.'

'OK, we give in. Who?'

'Well, Xanthe is Swedish, but went to school in Russia, and Gabriel spent years working in Africa for 'Médecins Sans Frontiers' before he came back here and swept her off her 'miguu'. That means 'feet' in Swahili.'

Rose nodded. 'I figured as much, but why is that an issue?'

'Well, it looks like our party of three has just become a party of five. They'll bring their wedding day forward and use the trip as their honeymoon. Are you guys up to another wedding? The one you did for me at Port Douglas went well, so you're getting good at them, aren't you?'

Rose shook her head. 'You know I tried it once and didn't like it, and Sandy hasn't been down that treacherous, tortuous toll road as yet.'

Nic nodded. 'Anyway, I'll be giving them the news tomorrow night. We're having dinner at the Stokehouse Restaurant in Southbank. Are you guys free?'

'Yes, we think so, but won't you feel uncomfortable meeting the man who's taken away the love of your lonely life?'

'Rose, it was over ten years ago, and I know he'll be good for her, and not just good enough. I'd met him at the Breakfast Creek Hotel as we were drowning our sorrows in a shared bottle of a Macallan Single Malt. He was new in town, looking for a job, and told me about the gig he had just finished in Africa working for Doctors Without Borders. Then he said he was having trouble getting a look at the local hospitals, so I gave him Xanthe's phone number.'

'Wow, our Nic Thorn is a matchmaker. Are you sure you're not a Jane Austen fan too? Have you ever read 'Emma'?

'Nope, but as for Jane Austen movies, Gwyneth Paltrow in Emma was outstanding. It should have won her the Oscar and not that silly Willy Shakespeare movie.'

Sandy grinned. 'Nic, you are an idiot.'

'I know, and Rose's parents keep telling her that. It's great, so as long as they keep thinking that I'm not a threat to steal her away from them.'

'Please steal me away from them, Nic....Oops, that came out wrong, didn't it?'

'Yep, you once told me we'll never marry, so you can't become Rose Thorn.'

'Yes, I did say that, but thought you'd forgotten.'

Nic went to stand up and Dog sensed the change. The cat raised his head and stared at him. 'OK, I guess I won't be moving for a while. Dog has me trapped. Just how much does this cat weigh?'

Sandy leaned over to pat the cat whilst Nic sat. 'About eight kilograms, but we like to keep him lean and hungry, just in case Rose's -ex turns up here again unannounced. So again, what's the latest with the Aged Care investigation?'

'Chewy hasn't got very far into that yet, but he managed to get hold of the Aged Care Budget Report. It's some fascinating reading if you're having trouble falling asleep. Are you either of you interested in having a look?

Rose nodded. 'Sandy did the books for 'The She Shed', so it couldn't be much more complicated than that? I assume it's just debtors, creditors, ledgers and labels, just in Government speak?'

'Yep, but the report is over one hundred pages long and has no pretty pictures.'

Sandy nodded, yawned, stood up and relocated from sitting in the deck chair to the soft Papasan. 'I'll have a look, send it to me.'

'I'll get Chewy to Express Post two copies and email one so you can upload it to your Kindle. It's a confidential report, so he'll have it hidden between the pages of another book.'

Rose sighed. 'So, what's next for us? Are you still OK with us working with you on these scam and fraud investigations? It seems there is an endless list of stuff you must look into.'

'Well, one of the other things on the horizon is looking into motor vehicle accident scams. The Motor Trade Association of South Australia, and one of the big Insurance players, wants us to take a closer look at them.'

'You said 'us' again, Nic.'

'Yep, you two are still part of Nic Thorn and Associates. Are you getting tired of it all yet? I haven't put you in too much danger, have I?'

Rose looked over to Sandy, but she'd fallen asleep in the Papasan. 'Me no, and I think I can speak for Sandy too, but maybe not for Dog.'

Nic smiled. 'The big test will be going overseas together. It will be easier as there are five of us, but I won't have access to my support networks like I have here.'

Rose sighed. 'If you're worried about it, we won't go. You promised, and we'll be very disappointed, but we won't go.'

Nic shrugged, then scooped up the cat and dropped him on Sandy's lap who woke up with a start. 'I wasn't asleep. I was listening with my eyes closed.'

Nic saluted and headed off into the night.

The following evening, Nic was waiting for Rose and Sandy by his basement carpark, waiting for Sandy and Rose to arrive for the dinner reservation at Stokehouse. They had told him they would drive over, so he would let them in to park underneath. A fully restored 1974 Jensen Interceptor drove slowly down the turnout and stopped beside him. The growl of the V8 engine reverberated in the small space.

Nic took a closer look and noticed Rose was driving. 'Where did you get this? Is it yours?'

Rose wound down the window and turned off the engine. 'I have just picked it up from the mechanic. It's been a little project of ours to restore it, then flip it.'

'So it *was* yours? But how? Where is your market?'

Rose looked at him. 'You may know stuff, do stuff, find stuff, and lose stuff, but we know stuff about people.' Nic grinned. 'Touché.'

Rose continued: 'We discovered the car a few months ago. It was in a storage facility. Then I was talking to one of our ladies who used to buy from our couture shop and remembered that her husband runs a Car Maintenance business in Milton. I chatted with them, and it didn't cost much to fully restore. Once word got around, it wasn't hard to on-sell.'

'Tell me more, but maybe over dinner. Let's get it into the basement and then we'll meet up with Xanthe and Gabriel. Before we do that though, can I ask a huge favour?'

Rose looked at him, and Nic grinned. 'Can I drive it into the carpark?'

Rose stepped out and held the door so he could climb in. Nic drove the car into the basement, parked it next to his Mustang, then pulled off his car cover and covered the Jensen. 'This should keep it away from prying eyes, but why you didn't offer to sell it to me?'

Rose shrugged. 'It's a one-of-a-kind, like me.'

They walked over to the nearby Stokehouse Restaurant and Nic approached the maître de. 'Reservation for five, The Thorn Party.'

The host nodded and led them over to their seats. Xanthe and Gabriel had not yet arrived.

Around thirty minutes later, there was a commotion at the front of the restaurant and Nic whispered to the others. 'That would be them.' Other guests in the restaurant appeared to step out of the way of the glamorous couple that had just entered. It was like the parting of the Red Sea.

They watched as the charming couple made their way over to them, and everyone in the restaurant was watching to see where they would eventually sit. An elderly Italian gentleman moved towards Xanthe, and she held out her hand. He kissed it lightly, uttered 'Bellissimo', and bowed as she passed. Rose whispered, 'Crikey Nic. I think they broke the mould when they made those two. How long has it been since you've seen them?'

Nic smiled. 'This is how the beautiful people live.'

Nic stood up, hugged Xanthe and then moved around to Gabriel. 'It's been a long time, Gabriel. Do you still favour the Macallan?'

'Yes, old man. It's been a while since we downed the last one. Ten years?' His accent was South African, with a French lilt. He had dark brooding eyes, thick dark wavy hair, and high cheekbones, and looked like a fashion model.

Sandy was holding her breath, then leaned towards Rose. 'He looks like a movie star.'

Rose nodded. 'Which one?'

'The one that plays Superman.'

'OK...but which Superman?'

'The recent ones. Henry something. I can't think of anything at the moment.'

Nic overheard and grinned. 'Let me introduce you to my business associates, Miss Sandy Fraser and Miss Rose Palmer.'

'Enchante.' Gabriel lightly kissed their hands, and Rose spoke first. 'Nic didn't mention to me you were French. He said that you were with Doctors Without Borders in Africa. Were you born in France?'

'Oui, mademoiselle.'

Sandy hadn't spoken yet as she was still trying to figure out what to say. Xanthe noticed. 'We won't bite Sandy. I don't know what Nic said about me, and yes, we parted. I stayed in the hospital with my broken legs and became a Doctor. It was over ten years ago, and he is all yours.'

Her accent was lightly Swedish, with a hint of an Australian accent.

Sandy chuckled. 'Nope, it's not like that, Xanthe. We both work with him.'

'Yes, I know that. It's just that he is well....'

Nic took over the conversation before she could finish. 'So Xanthe, did you stay in General Practice or move into a specialist field? You don't post on Facebook, so I've lost touch.'

'It's paediatrics now, Nic. I've got a chance to become the Head of Paediatric Surgeons with the Brisbane Children's Hospital, so I'm just biding my time to see how that unfolds. Gabriel is still studying and wants to go back to Africa. Doctors Without Borders are always looking for help. What about you?'

'Well, I'm still freelancing with the investigations stuff. It's been well over ten years, and it still gets me out of bed in the morning, so that's good. I met Rose on a dating site. She needed a '+1' for a funeral, and then she introduced me to her BFF Sandy. I've been dragging them around Australia with all my stuff, and they put up with me.'

Gabriel hailed a waiter and ordered a bottle of Dom Perignon. 'So Nic, did you sort out the thing with the Australian Security Intelligence Organisation? Last I heard, you were still trying to prove your innocence.'

Rose and Sandy glanced at Nic whilst he considered the response: 'Not yet, mate. It's still a work in progress, but it's not stopping me from doing my thing. They still use me from time to time.'

Rose could sense that Nic was uncomfortable with the topic, so she raised the matter of the recent car renovation. 'So Nic, did you like what we did to the Jensen Interceptor? It was Uncle Alberts, but there was no mention of it in his will reading. Father was cleaning out all Albert's stuff under their house and found a receipt and a key to a Storage Unit in Milton.'

Gabriel was listening in. 'What year? They made them with steel instead of aluminium for a couple of years. I have a friend who has one. Are you keeping it or selling it?'

Rose continued. 'He told me that I was welcome to have whatever was inside. It was mainly old vinyl records and a couple of filing cabinets. Stuff that he didn't store under my parents' home in Hamilton. We were surprised at how wide the unit was, and then the Storage Centre Manager asked us if we needed the forklift to remove the car. We said, 'What car?'

Gabriel interjected again. 'I'll give you five thousand more for whatever you sold it for.' Rose shook her head, 'Sorry, Gabriel, it's already been sold. I've promised it to someone, and my word is my bond.'

Nic looked over at Rose and smiled. 'You're not going to let me forget that, are you?'

Nic turned to Xanthe. 'The first time I met Rose, and she agreed to work with me on one of my investigations. I made her pirouette through a waterfall at the Gallery of Modern Art in Brisbane. It's still sort of a sore point.'

'How long ago was that Rose?'

Rose nodded. 'Nearly two years already. I needed Nic for the +1 thing for Uncle Albert's funeral. Sandy and I have stayed around ever since.'

Sandy changed the topic. 'Tell us about the diamond, Gabriel. Nic said you won it on a TV Game Show, and it's not what it's supposed to be.'

'Yes, that's the case. It was one of those new Game Shows. We were filming the pilot, and I was allowed to keep the prize. I didn't think they did that unless the show went to air, but never mind. When I turned over the two matching panels, the ring was there. I looked at Xanthe, and she nodded. I assumed it was to marry me, not just take the ring. It was either that or the set of steak knives.'

Xanthe laughed. 'You didn't tell me that.'

Gabriel continued. 'Anyway, when I got it valued after the show, instead of being worth around fifty thousand, it's come back under three.'

Rose piped up. 'What about the Diamond Certification?'

'Yes, we have that too. That's where it started. I showed the show's producers the certificate, and they told me it was not their problem. They didn't pay for the prize, as it was part of the advertising agreement from the supplier.'

Xanthe took over. 'So, with Nic's help, we want to find out what happened, and if it takes us to Russia or Africa, we don't mind. We're both overdue for an overseas holiday.'

Suddenly, a young woman came up to their table. 'I'm so sorry to interrupt, but can I please take a picture with you, Mr Cavill?'

'Sure, little lady.' Nic stood up, and the young woman stared at him, then shook her head, so Nic clarified his offer. 'Sorry, I meant I'll take the picture for you, besides, my name is Bruce Wayne, not Mr Cavill.'

'Oh, OK.' The young woman kept standing there, however, a little confused.

Gabriel stood up and moved around to have the picture taken, and the young woman moved away. He sat down again and Sandy looked at him. 'Does that happen often? Being mistaken for Superman?'

'Not really; I feel sorry for the other guy as he must always be mistaken for Dr. Gabriel Goodenough.'

The waiter returned and offered to refill their champagne glasses. 'I'm so sorry about that.'

Gabriel nodded. 'That's fine. I'm glad there are no ABBA fans here as Xanthe often gets mistaken for Agnetha.' The group laughed, and Rose continued: 'So when are you guys getting married? Nic mentioned you were bringing the ceremony forward and will use the trip overseas as your honeymoon.'

Xanthe smiled. 'It's tonight, Rose, and we need a favour. Would you be our witness?'

Rose smiled. 'You're serious?'

Gabriel responded. 'Yes. Xanthe's family are stranded on a Cruise Ship in the Greek Islands. They were supposed to be flying in tomorrow, but the ship has struck the ground in the Mediterranean, so they are all being evacuated to Athens. My parents are both deceased, so only my brother will be attending. He's due to meet us here in about an hour.'

'What about the Celebrant?'

They looked over at Nic. 'Hey, don't look at me. I'm giving the bride away.'

The group had finished their meals and were standing on the external wooden decking area of the restaurant, facing the river. The backdrop was the well-lit Goodwill Bridge and a view of the Brisbane Central Business District. The best man was late, and so was the Celebrant. It was now nearing 11 p.m., and the roar of a speed boat from the river broke the silence. Gabriel waved to the occupant and looked around. 'Well, at least they've arrived, Xanthe.'

The boat moored at the grassy area nearby; two men climbed out and started running towards the restaurant. Both were dressed in dark suits and struggled to run on the now dewy grass. One slipped and fell onto his knees. He rolled onto his back and cried out in frustration.

Xanthe looked down at the calamity. 'I wonder what their hurry is.'

The two men reached the cement promenade, stopped, and looked around. The second man removed his jacket, swung it around his head, and sat on the nearest bench. Sandy looked down at them. 'Don't they know where they are going?'

'Who?'

'Those two men. Didn't you tell them where the restaurant is?'

'Probably, but those two aren't with us. Gabriel's brother arrived a couple of minutes ago. He's at the front bar, and The Celebrant is the Head Chef.'

5

A young man ambled over from the front bar, he was wearing designer jeans, a pale blue paisley shirt, and a purple dinner jacket. There was a single silver pewter rose in his lapel and a small sapphire in his left ear. The Head Chef had tidied himself up and walked to their small gathering. 'Ladies and Gentlemen, I will be conducting the service tonight. Are we all ready to commence proceedings?'

Nic nodded and led Xanthe away to make her re-entrance as the incoming bride-to-be. Gabriel's brother came up, introduced himself to Rose, and shook hands with his brother. 'Yo Gabe. Are you ready?'

'Yes, thanks, Marcel. Let's do this. Nic will be giving Xanthe away. This is Rose, the other witness.'

A small table was set up at the end of the deck, and the Celebrant moved towards it. He then nodded to the gathered crowd and announced that the formalities were due to begin. 'La vie en Rose' began softly playing through the sound system.

Sandy and a waiter held up a white ribbon for the bride to break at the commencement of her short walk toward wedded bliss, paying homage to the French tradition. Nic and Xanthe were now back at the deck entrance, and he nodded to the Celebrant.

Xanthe broke the white ribbon and moved towards Gabriel. The ceremony was short and uncomplicated. They both said, 'Je le veux' at the appropriate moment and then the Croquembouche was served.

It was simple and elegant.

When the service ended, they went to the Brisbane River, where a gondola was waiting for them. They rode in it across to the other side, and a helicopter took them away into the night sky.

Rose took a breath. 'Wow. Hey Sandy, remind me where we can find a French-born, South African-bred Doctor that whisks you away in his helicopter on your wedding night.'

'Have you been back on the Vita Brevis dating site lately? Look under 'M' for Médecins, although I've already tried 'FD' for French Doctor, but it didn't get a result.'

'Oh, did you ask Gabriel why he waved at the men from the speed boat?'

'Yes. He said he wasn't waving, he was brushing a bug from his face. It was a big bug.' Nic and Marcel then approached them. 'Hey Sandy, have you met Marcel? He's French and a Doctor in the Air Force.'

Sandy looked at Rose, then back at Nic. 'Bonjour um, Marcel. Sorry, that's about the extent of my French. Rose speaks French, though.'

'It's all good, Sandy. I'm an Aussie, born in Bondi and grew up there, and yep, I'm a Fighter pilot in the Air Force, but I'm a Doctor of Mathematics, not the sick people stuff like Gabe and Xanthe.'

Sandy grinned. 'Good to know, Marcel. Anyway, it's late and well past our bedtime. If we don't leave here soon, we'll all turn into pumpkins. So it's good night from us.'

'And good night from him.' Nic commented as they watched Marcel walk away. 'He's staying at the Mantra Hotel in Grey Street, about a ten-minute walk from here. What about you guys? Are you taking the Jensen, or will you leave it here until tomorrow and take an Uber?'

'We've already organised the Uber. So, when are we catching up with the amazing Doctors' Goodenough again?'

'In a couple of days. They've got a couple of nights at the Palazzo Versace down at the Gold Coast, then the games afoot.'

'Russia or Africa?'

'I still don't know yet.'

'That's going to make it an expensive plane ticket then.'

'Nup, I've booked five tickets on both airlines for Thursday. I can exchange them for an upgrade.'

Rose laughed. 'So I'll have to pay you back instead of the airlines. That suits me. Will you take a payment plan, say, over ten years?'

'Wow, Rose, does that mean you will be around for another ten years until you pay it off?'

Rose shook her head. 'Err, maybe not. Will you accept a personal cheque?'

They headed down to the turnout at Nic's apartment complex, and an Uber was waiting for them. 'See you in the morning.'

Sandy nodded. 'Sure, but it's already morning, so how about making it this afternoon around two at our place? Has the Aged Care Report arrived yet?'

'I'm expecting it tomorrow and will personally deliver it to you along with the Jensen.' Rose handed him the keys. 'That will work. Then you can follow us when we deliver it to the new owner tomorrow afternoon. See you then.'

Just before 2 p.m., Nic arrived in the Jensen. He wiped down the duco, rubbed over the seat, stepped out, and started to spray the windows with a water bottle. Rose and Sandy were watching him and Sandy whispered. 'You know Nic will make someone very happy one day. If he only spoke French and was a Doctor, he might be a great catch.'

Sandy called out to him. 'Stop that. You're making too much noise.'

Nic looked up, threw the polishing cloth towards them, then walked over and handed Sandy the copy of the Aged Care Report. 'Have fun reading this.'

'Thanks, Nic.' Sandy took a quick flick through the binder. 'What, no pretty pictures? Not even a single pie graph or anything?'

'Nup, but make sure you keep it safe. It's not for public viewing.'

Sandy took it inside, and they waited for her to return.

Meantime, Nic had retrieved the polishing cloth and started rubbing the timber beams on the side of the house with it. 'So, where are we taking the car?'

'Down to Tennyson, near the Pat Rafter Tennis Arena.'

'OK. Have you checked out the new owner? Will they be good for the payment?'

'Yes, Nic.'

'Do they need to meet you at a Bank or anything to make the payment transfer?'

'No, Nic.'

'Have they already paid then?'

'Yes, Nic, and Nic, please stop asking so many questions. You have to trust people sometimes.'

'I trust you are all over this, but can I still drive it?'

'Sure, we're doing an exchange anyway. I'll get you to drive the trade car back.'

Sandy returned, and they drove through a few suburbs eventually stopping outside a stately property facing the Brisbane River on King Arthur Terrace in Tennyson. The cast iron gates were open so Rose directed Nic to drive into the driveway. He stepped out of the car and waited for them.

'I know this place. It's where my clients Douglas and Elliott live. Have you sold the Jensen to my clients? No wonder Douglas didn't upgrade to the Maybach. He was buying your Jensen.'

'Not quite. This car is a present for Elliott's wife. It's their forty-fifth wedding anniversary today.'

'Really? I didn't know he was married.'

'That's right. You might buy stuff and sell stuff, lose stuff, and find stuff, but we know stuff about people. In this case, we know your people are also our people.'

'My people are now your people. I must have missed that in a memo somewhere.'

Elliott and Douglas came out of the house. Nic had brokered purchases for their extensive car collections. They all hugged and made small talk about the Jensen. 'Thanks to your ladies here, my wife is now the proud owner of a Jensen Interceptor. I couldn't believe it when I heard a rumour that a fully restored one was available in Brisbane. I made a few calls, and my people talked to your people, and now I have it.'

'Sorry, Elliott, this was all Rose and Sandy, nothing to do with me.'

'Well, you have taught them well, kind sir.'

Elliott handed Rose a set of keys. 'Your next project awaits, young lady.' There was a 1954 Morgan + 4 sitting in the driveway. The paintwork was a little worse for wear, and the interior trim looked shabby.

'I've been offered twenty thousand for this little one. Its condition is listed as fair, but with a little of that fairy dust you will sprinkle over it, you should double your investment.'

Elliott helped Nic climb into the little sports car. 'I hope you've got a handkerchief to put over your mouth, young man. Otherwise, you'll eat a few g-nats on your way back g-home.'

Nic drove off, and Rose and Sandy followed him in their car.

It was around 5 when they returned to West End and Dog was patiently waiting for them. This time, he had a friend although it was a lot smaller, about one-tenth the size, but had almost the same black and white markings, and a matching fluffy fur coat.

Nic drove the Morgan into the garage under the house, came around to the back deck and noticed the animals. 'Oh no, just what have you been up to, Dog?'

Sandy nodded. 'Don't worry, it's not a cat. We think it's a Pomeranian, a Geranium, or a Tea-Cup dog. Something like that.'

'A Geranium is a plant, Sandy. There's one in the front garden next door.'

'I guess so. It might be from there anyway, Dave, the neighbour from next door, mentioned he was looking after a dog.'

'I don't think that's a dog. It's a mini-me Maine Coon cat.'

They were watching Dog, and wherever he went, the tiny little dog trotted along behind. Nic then watched the cat move off to take the back stairs off the deck, but the little dog found the risers too high, so it jumped down each step, one at a time. 'So what is the tiny dog then? I don't think 'Tea Cup' is a breed. Is it fully grown?'

Rose nodded. 'It's a miniature Pekingese. They grow to about twenty centimetres We have to keep an eye on it, but it's worth about four thousand dollars.' Dave, the neighbour, came around the side of the house. 'Have you guys seen Goliath? Or is he still playing hooky with Dog?'

Nic laughed. 'That tiny little dog, no bigger than my last sneeze, is called Goliath?'

Rose grinned. 'Yep, David *and* Goliath live next door to us, so beware any burglars or door-to-door salesman.'

Sandy called out. 'They went under the house. Dave, please try to keep Goliath away from the kitty-dins as we don't want him exploding from overeating.'

Rose was setting down the ordered pizzas for dinner and serving the drinks when her phone rang and she looked at it. 'This won't be good.'

Nic looked over at her. 'Why?'

'Well, I only have about ten numbers. So, whoever it is, it will not be good.'

Rose picked up the phone. 'This is Rose.'

Rose paused to listen to the caller. 'Thank you for letting me know. I appreciate it.' Rose disconnected the call and looked over at Nic. 'I've just been offered the role of an Aged Care Compliance Officer.'

'Oops, I forgot to tell you about that. At least you have some time to learn the ropes. I told them you had to give six weeks' notice to your current employer.' Rose looked at him. 'But I'm not working at the moment.'

'You work with me, and I have a stringent policy regarding the termination of all my employees.'

Rose shrugged. 'What's it all about? Is Sandy working with me, too?'

'Sort of. You're on the inside working with the small team of Internal Auditors, whereas Sandy and I are coming in as External Auditors. We'll be working together, but not together.'

'You're doing it again, Nic, not making sense, but making sense. Get it together.'

'Sorry, Rose, and by the way, do you want to see your new Aged Care ID Card? I have it here on my phone, ready to be scanned.'

'Sure.'

Nic held out his phone: It was a headshot of Rose however, her shoulder-length Auburn hair had been shortened into a bob-cut, and she was wearing black 'Buddy Holly' style reading glasses.

'Is that supposed to be me? And what's with the name? I can't be Rosa Giardino; that is ridiculous.'

Sandy looked at the photo, smiled and started googling on her phone. 'I can see where you got your inspiration from, Nic.' She showed him, then Rose. It was one of the female characters from the Scooby Doo film franchise.

'He's made you into a Velma. It's the same coloured hair, the same bob haircut and black-rimmed glasses. You'll fit right in as a genuine Scooby Doo investigator.'

Rose sighed. 'Damn you, Nic.' Then explained to Sandy that 'Rosa Giardino' could be loosely translated from Italian into "Rose Garden".

A couple of days later, the Goodenoughs had returned from their little vacation down at the Gold Coast, and everyone was gathered around the dining table at Nic's apartment. Gabriel nodded as he looked around. 'Nice digs, my man. Xanthe gave all of this up and went with someone good enough instead?'

'I wasn't living here back then. After Xanthe left me, I was deployed to Afghanistan. I spent most of the time just trying to keep myself alive and the rest of the time wondering where my life was heading. I'd heard Xanthe was studying to be a Doctor. I got captured and smashed up, but she wasn't my Doctor when I returned home.' Rose and Sandy had heard a little about Nic's exploits and were interested in discovering more. He was still very guarded about the experiences.

Nic continued: 'It was a dangerous place to be, especially once some of my buddies discovered I was on a somewhat different mission than they were. When I was rescued, I went off to special confinement and the guys wanted to know why I was being looked after differently. Someone mentioned that I was aligned with ASIO, and the fan got splattered with the messy brown stuff.'

Xanthe took a small sip of her wine. 'I heard you found out it was someone higher up the food chain, and you didn't like that. Something about being a sacrificial lamb?'

Rose looked at Nic. 'My parents used the same thing with me. I had to marry a short, fat, and shallow Accountant so my father could win a business deal. My marriage lasted three days, but somehow, it's insignificant compared to what Nic went through.'

'Thanks, Rose, but I don't think you almost punched your father in the face or threatened him in the presence of some important people, including an ex-Prime Minister.'

'Not quite. Sandy came with me on my honeymoon instead. We got a little drunk and sang karaoke badly in a bar in Auckland. That was about it.'

Nic continued. 'Someone even higher up the food chain helped Chewy and I set up the scambusting business, and ten years later I'm Batman, working with a real-life Robin and Cat-woman.'

Sandy grinned. 'When do we get our little masks and cool motorbikes?'

'I'm working on it. Besides, we're on this diamond caper now, and the Batcave is undergoing major renovations.'

6

Nic pulled up a roll of paper and flattened it on the table. It was a world map with red lines crisscrossing the continents. A picture of Xanthe's hand with the diamond ring was centred in Australia.

'We've tracked the shipment of diamonds into Australia. It came via Dubai and was originally from Botswana, East Africa. So, guys pack your bag as it looks like we're off to Africa.'

Gabriel grinned. 'Helpful, as I've got a dual passport, and Xanthe and I can use the trip for a honeymoon.'

Nic nodded. 'What about your shots, though? Are they all up to date? Yellow Fever and all that stuff?'

'Yes, we both keep our immunisations up to date.'

Nic looked over towards the others. 'How about you two guys?'

'Yep.' And with that, Rose and Sandy handed over receipts from a Travel Doctor's clinic. Nic looked at them, rolled them into two paper balls and threw them down the corridor toward his bedroom. 'Consider them presented for payment. I'll file them later. Pick that up, Ivy.'

A door opened within the wall, and a robotic vacuum emerged. It folded out an arm from its lid, scooped the paper balls up, and disappeared into the wall. They all kept watching for something else to happen.

It didn't although someone uttered: 'Wow, what was that thing? I'm a sucker for a good vacuum cleaner.'

Nic turned back. 'That was terrible, Rose, and you reckon my Dad jokes are bad.' Rose shook her head. 'That was Xanthe, not me. When do we leave?'

'In four days, on Sunday morning. We're taking a flight to Dubai, staying a couple of days, and then another flight to Nairobi. We could've flown direct, but I have some people to catch up with in the UAE. They want to do a meet and greet and thank me for shutting down a wine scammer.'

Sandy nodded. 'Hey, we helped you out with that, Nic. Whatever happened to the phoney Lord Somersby-Kent and his son?'

Nic responded. 'They're both doing jail time in Perth, last I heard. So yes, you can meet with my people in Dubai. We might even meet someone from the Dubai Royal Family, so you could kiss a real prince and turn him into a real frog.'

Nic then went over the remainder of the plan: 'OK. You won the trip with me but only met me before the show. We are not close friends, and you don't know much about me. Xanthe and Gabriel will be on their honeymoon, and you have all known each other for years, but have lost touch. I've compiled a dossier that you can all read over the next few days. I'll be travelling alone, and if I get into trouble, you can go ahead without me.'

Gabriel nodded. 'Are you expecting trouble?'

'I'm never sure when travelling overseas. My previous connections might have a legacy issue. It's been over ten years, but I won't know until I get there.'

Rose looked over to Nic. 'So all the stuff Sandy and I were loading on you about not taking us overseas was legitimate?'

'Sort of. It's just about being careful, being invisible and keeping a low profile, but travelling with two Western women and two Doctors might raise my profile.'

Rose nodded. 'I think I get it now, here in Australia, you can rely on your networks, but being overseas changes the dynamics.'

'Yep, and some people, in certain countries, own big elephants with long memories.' Nic folded the sheet of paper and handed over the dossiers with the plane tickets. 'There's good news and bad news. The good news is that we are all flying Business Class.' He paused for effect. 'And the bad news is....the departure time is two a.m. Oh, and it's about a fourteen-hour flight.'

Rose sighed. 'Damn you, long-haul airlines.'

Nic grinned. 'OK, let's wind this up and meet again at the International Airport Terminal. Remember, we don't have to check in simultaneously; just be there at least three hours before flight time.'

It was around 11 p.m. when Rose and Sandy arrived at the Brisbane International Airport. They had decided to dress for the occasion as they were flying Business Class and turned out in their favourite couture outfits. They were standing in the check-in queue when suddenly movement and noise broke the late-night silence.

Sandy whispered to Rose. 'Xanthe and Gabriel have arrived, and the paparazzi are in tow this time. It must be so terrifying being chased all your life just for being beautiful.'

'Well, we scrub up all right, and as they're travelling with us, we might even turn up in the latest 'No Idea' magazine too. Should we help them with their luggage?'

Sandy shook her head. 'It doesn't look like we're needed, as they've found a use for those pesky, persistent paparazzi.'

They watched as three photographers were helping with the luggage, and two others were still fawning over Xanthe, trying to get a picture. They were ushered straight to the front of the First Class counter and handed over their passports and tickets. Sandy shrugged. 'I thought Nic said we were all going Business Class?'

Rose sighed. 'So did I? Did you read Nic's portfolio about Xanthe and Gabriel? She's still getting offers from International modelling agencies. I think it's going to be an interesting trip.'

'We've done modelling too, Sandy.'

Sandy pulled up a picture on her phone. 'I know, but she does look a little like a young version of Agnetha from ABBA.'

Rose whispered. 'Mamma-Mia, here we go again.'

Finally, Gabriel noticed Sandy and Rose in the other queue and beckoned them over. 'Ladies, over this way, please. We have all been upgraded, so we don't have to wait.' Rose whispered. 'It seems like your whole life is an upgrade, Gabriel.'

'What's that, Rose?'

'Nothing, Dr Goodenough. Thank you for letting us know.'

Sandy helped her with the luggage, and they moved out of the line to the First Class counter and provided their details. Rose whispered. 'Have you seen Nic?'

Xanthe shook her head. 'No, but he'll be around somewhere. He's always late.'

Rose and Sandy looked at each other. 'The Nic that we know is never late. We've only seen it once, and that was when he was playing a role as our Executive Assistant.'

'To both of you?'

'Yes, we could both tell him what to do and where to go, but he didn't listen as he kept coming back for more directions.'

They collected the passports, printed tickets from the attendant and headed downstairs to the Business Class Lounge. Nic still had not arrived. They were sitting together in the Lounge when another attendant came up and handed out the International Travel Declaration forms.

Xanthe and Gabriel started to complete theirs, however, Sandy and Rose had just begun reading the document. 'What's wrong? Don't you have a pen?'

Rose shook her head. 'That's not the issue, Xanthe. We currently don't have employment and are mainly working with Nic. I don't think he'd appreciate us putting 'Nic Thorn and Associates' on the declaration, along with 'fraud and scam busters' as our occupation.' They eventually declared themselves self-employed business operators of 'The

She Shed,' handed over their travel forms and boarded the plane.

Nic was still not around.

Around fourteen hours later, they arrived in Dubai. Sandy and Rose made their way through customs, collected their luggage, and saw Xanthe and Gabriel in the queue. Rose nodded to them. 'Have you guys seen Nic?'

Gabriel shook his head. 'Nope, but I sent a message to Chewy when we were in the Lounge, and he confirmed he was at the Brisbane airport, so he'll be here somewhere. There is a tracker in his watch.'

They moved away as they were called forward to have their travel papers processed, and Xanthe called back. 'We didn't see him on the plane either. I wonder if he sat in Economy.'

Sandy and Rose were called forward, completed their paperwork, and waited for them. 'Here they come, Rose. Don't they both look like they just turned up from leaving their house, not after a fourteen-hour flight from Brisbane? We freshened up before landing, so why don't we look that good?'

Gabriel greeted them. 'Wow, that was a pretty easy process as the Saudis have excellent facilities here. Where are you guys staying?'

Rose held up an accommodation voucher. 'About one minute away in the nearest Airport Hotel as we're only here for a few days. What about you two?'

Xanthe smiled. 'The Burj Khalifa, on the eleventh floor, although we have access to the viewing deck on the one hundred and forty-eighth.'

They waited for another twenty minutes in the customs area but were requested to move along by security, so they decided to find an airport bar to wait for Nic. They found seats and ordered light meals and drinks.

Gabriel's phone chirped. 'Well, that's good. Nic is somewhere in the Dubai airport. Chewy sent me a link to his watch locator. It's showing he's here but he's not moving. The signal is not strong enough to get within two hundred metres, so he must be getting close.'

7

They spent time talking about the flight and movies they watched, and eventually, Rose had to ask about their fresh appearance. 'We both showered and changed clothes on the plane. How come you two look so fresh and vibrant?'

Xanthe smiled. 'We used their onboard Beauty Spa Treatment service. Sorry, we thought you knew?'

'Damn you, Nic.'

'What's that, Rose?'

'Well, Nic could have told us before we boarded.'

Xanthe continued. 'Anyway, did you get much sleep?'

Rose shook her head. 'No, I watched three movies, but Sandy managed to sleep for ten hours, and woke up with two hours to go. I pointed out to her she'd been asleep ten hours and we only had two hours of flight time left.'

Gabriel grinned. 'Lucky you, Sandy. Which movies?' Rose continued: 'I assume Nic told you about the Aged Care fraud thing we are looking into when we return. Well, he's given me the name Rosa Giardino, and even set me up with an ID, and I look like Velma from the Scooby Doo cartoon TV series. It was made into a real live-action movie in 2002. I found that and watched it. Freddie Prinze and the actress who played Buffy in the TV series were in it, and I do look like Thelma. It's so embarrassing.'

Rose showed them her Aged Care ID, and they all laughed.

Gabriel's phone chirped again and showed Nic was getting closer. They tidied up the plates and drinks, settled the bill, and stood outside the restaurant to look out for him. Sandy saw him first flanked by two Airport Security Officers. Nic made eye contact and moved towards his group. The Security Officers slowed their walks to allow him to gain a little distance from them.

'Hi guys, sorry I'm late, something's come up.'

Sandy and Rose moved towards him, but he held his hands in front to tell them not to come closer. He eventually stopped about a metre away.

Rose took the lead. 'We didn't see you on the plane.'

'Nope.'

'Were you in First Class?'

'Nope.'

'Cattle Class? Up the back with the unaccompanied children?'

'Nope.'

'Come on, Nic; you weren't up the pointy end with the Captain?'

He laughed. 'Nope, but you're not supposed to see me anyway.' He opened his jacket pocket and withdrew a folded black wallet, flipped it open, and it revealed "Nic Thorn Air Security Officer."'

Xanthe looked at it. 'You were the Flight Marshall. Wow, that's a step up even for you. Did you carry a gun?'

Nic shook his head. 'No gun. When I checked in at Brisbane Airport, the Chief ASO asked me if I could do it as the guy allocated to the board had to bail at short notice. His wife was due to give birth, and complications set in. They had checked me out and told me that as my ASIO clearance was still current, I could stand in. I also knew the pilot that helped, but now there's a wrinkle.'

Gabriel nodded back at the Airport officers. 'I assume they are the wrinkle?'

'Yep. It looks like re-instating my ASIO status was brought to the attention of some people here in Dubai, so they are effectively putting me under house arrest until the matter can be resolved. They think I'm a spy.'

Rose nodded. 'What do you want us to do about the diamond stuff then?'

'Nothing. Just remember you are all here as tourists. See the sights, do touristy stuff, and don't worry about me. It will be sorted out. Hey Rose, have you shown the others your Scooby Doo ID card yet?'

Rose sighed. 'Yes, I have.'

Nic nodded again. 'So, you guys can take on the personas of Fred, Daphne, Shaggy, and Velma. See the sights of Dubai without me until it's sorted out, but please do not start any Scooby Doo investigations. Maybe get Xanthe to show you the indoor Ice Rink at the Dubai Mall.'

Xanthe nodded. 'I'm good with that and still have my unlimited pass, given that I made the Swedish Olympic Team in the day. It's about one of the only perks I have left.'

The two Security Officers came forward. 'We have to go, sir.'

Nic turned around. 'Thank you for letting me advise my travelling party. I assume you have their details and will contact them once this matter is sorted. Our party is expected to be travelling onto Africa in four days.'

The lead officer responded. 'Yes, we understand; however, that is not your concern.'

Nic nodded, and was led away.

The group watched him leave through a 'No Entry' door, and Xanthe was the first to speak. 'What do we do know then? We have a car waiting outside, It can take you to your Hotel, or would you prefer to relocate to ours?'

Rose shook her head. 'No, but thanks for the offer. The Terminus Train will take us to our Hotel, about five minutes away. How about we get settled, catch up on some jet lag sleep, and meet at the Ice Rink in about five hours? All the Hotels have courtesy buses that will deliver the passengers there.'

'That works for us. Thanks, Rose.' Their group went outside to find the car.

A driver was waiting alongside a stretched white Hummer, holding a sign. 'Is-this Goodenough?'

They laughed when they saw it, and Gabriel smiled. 'I guess that's our car.'

Gabriel and Xanthe climbed in and noticed their luggage had been collected and was stored in the vehicle. 'Have you two seen inside one of these? Are you sure you don't want a ride to your Hotel next door?'

Rose shook her head. 'We've been there, done that. Besides, we can see our Hotel sign just down the street, and I don't think your driver would agree to take us, as it's too close.'

'Fair enough, we'll see you in about five hours.'

The Hummer merged into traffic, and Sandy and Rose returned to the terminal to make arrangements. They collected their luggage from the airport concierge and took the train to their

Hotel. 'This is five-star Sandy, and yet the Burj Khalifa is seven-star. What else do they get for the money?'

Sandy grinned. 'Only one thing I can think of. A bigger bill at checkout time.'

Five hours later, Rose and Sandy, caught the courtesy bus to the Dubai Mall and located the indoor Ice Rink. Ravel's Bolero was lightly playing through the centre's overhead sound system, and they were watching two skaters doing an impromptu version of the Jane Torvill and Christopher Dean performance from the 1984 Olympics.

'I bet that's them, Sandy.'

'Who?' Rose turned around, and Xanthe was standing beside her.

'Thanks, Rose, if you thought that was Gabriel and me, but he has two left feet. I got him onto the ice once, but he only pushed the penguin around.' Xanthe pointed towards a group of children, who were all propelling an upright plastic penguin to assist with their balance.

They were laughing as Gabriel arrived with three ice cream cones, and handed them one each.

'What's up? I assume from your laughing that Xanthe told you I can't skate. I grew up in South Africa, and there's not much ice there apart from the top of Table Mountain in winter.'

Rose nodded. 'But didn't your family relocate from France?'

'Well, yes, but I managed to avoid the winters, they're too cold. So, are we up for exploring the shopping in Dubai?'

Sandy looked at him. 'Let us get this straight, Xanthe. He's a Doctor, speaks fluent French and Swahili, is good-looking and likes going shopping?'

They found a coffee shop, ordered, took their seats and Sandy was about to explain their history with Nic when a well-dressed man approached them. He was in his early sixties and stood at the end of their table to gain their attention.

'Are you with the Nic Thorn party?'

They looked at him, and Rose responded. 'We could be, maybe, but what is this all about?'

'My name is Stewart Humphrey, and I'm from the Australian Consulate here in Dubai. I believe your friend is in a little bit of trouble.'

Rose stood up. 'Sorry, we can't confirm or deny that. Besides, how did you track us down? This shopping mall is huge.'

'I have my ways and would like to discuss the situation somewhere, a little less public if I may. So, perhaps at my office, we can talk more freely. Dubai can be a little .....I can keep you safe from the others.'

Rose looked around. 'What others? Are they your others, our others, or Nic's others from another other?' He leaned in closer and had the sweet aroma of Bulgari. 'You must be Rose.'

'I am. This is Sandy Fraser and Doctors Gabriel and Xanthe Goodenough. We're here on holiday and then heading off to Africa. Nic is most likely having his holiday without us.'

'Are you still intending on tracking down the diamond scammers?' The man then nodded toward Xanthe's diamond engagement ring. 'I've been talking with Chewy, Nic's confidant in Melbourne. That is not something I suggest that you pursue as it is very dangerous. I am not at liberty to discuss anything more and would strongly advise against it. Can I suggest we meet tomorrow at eleven a.m.? I will arrange for your transport.'

Gabriel shook his head. 'We have a driver. He'll know where your office is.'

'Fine. I will collect Rose and Sandy from their Hotel at ten thirty.'

The man walked off, leaving them bewildered by their situation. Gabriel shrugged. 'More shopping, or shall we call it quits and return to our Hotels?'

Rose looked at him. 'I think we've already had enough of the Scooby Doo mystery stuff, Gabriel. How about we have an early night and meet at the Consulate tomorrow to understand what Nic has got himself into.'

Gabriel stood up. 'Maybe not quite yet for me Are you coming, Xanthe?'

They parted ways, and the Goodenough party headed towards another shoe emporium, while Rose and Sandy returned to the Hotel.

Rose and Sandy arrived at their Hotel, where another man greeted them. He was dressed in the same elegant attire as Mr Humphrey and said he was from the South African Consulate. 'Ladies, I believe that you met with Stewart Humphrey at the Dubai Mall. I'm here to tell you to be careful.' He then put his Business Card on the concierge counter and walked away. They ignored it.

'This is getting interesting, isn't it, Rose?'

'Not the word I would use unless we discover what is happening. Nic could need our help. It would be the first time we've needed to work something out for ourselves instead of following his lead.'

'Yes. Are you scared, Rose?'

'Yes. Damn you, Nic.'

They went to their suite and ordered room service for dinner. Neither of them could eat much of the meal, so they decided on an early night and tried to catch up on some sleep.

It didn't work.

At 6 a.m., they used the rooftop pool for a swim. Sandy dipped her toe in the water, then withdrew it. 'Is this supposed to be heated?'

'I don't think so. It's already thirty-five degrees, so the pool water doesn't get a chance to cool down overnight.'

They dove in anyway and ordered a couple of iced orange juices from the pool bar. 'What do you think we should do about Nic?'

'Well, what we don't do is get into the car with Mr Humphrey. We'll follow him in a taxi if we have to, I'd feel more comfortable doing that.'

'Agreed. Let's go for a run and then get breakfast.'

'Breakfast, yes, run, no. This body doesn't run in thirty-five-degree heat.'

'Mine either. I hoped that you were listening and not just hung up on saving Nic.'

Rose sighed. 'Nope. I didn't bring my Bat-girl disguise with me, so I won't be able to without your help.'

'Good to know.'

8

After breakfast they changed into more serious attire, and waited for Stewart Humphrey to arrive. The man was right on time and showed them outside to the waiting car. 'Ladies.' He directed them to a White Toyota Land Cruiser. 'Sorry, but we would prefer to follow you in a taxi if that is all right.' He nodded. 'Understood, but here's a tip for the wary travellers: always take the second taxi here in Dubai; they are more likely to take you where you need to go and not where they want you to go to get you there.'

Sandy laughed. 'Have you been talking to Nic this morning? As that sounds like the sort of advice he would give.'

The well-dressed man smiled. 'Ah, Nic Thorn. He is an enigma, isn't he?'

Rose nodded. 'So, you do know him?'

'Yes, our paths have crossed over the years. I spent some time with him in Afghanistan during the war. I was lucky and managed to get out before it went crazy, but no more questions here, please.' He handed their taxi driver a Business Card, and they followed him to the Australian Embassy.

They drove through the gates, and Xanthe and Gabriel were waiting outside when they arrived. The driver stopped the car so Mr Humphrey could greet them.

'This way, please, ladies and gentlemen.'

The group followed him through the corridors, ending up in an ample office space. A framed portrait of Queen Elizabeth II hung on one wall; on the other was a photograph of the Australian Parliament House in Canberra. Rose nodded at the picture. 'Is that your house back in Sydney, Mr Humphrey?'

'Not quite, Miss Palmer, but I still have an office in there that you are welcome to use if you ever find yourself lost in the building and need a bathroom in a hurry. Please take a seat, and can I offer any of you a light beverage?'

The group requested chilled water and it was served promptly by the attendants dressed in the local attire. The attendants left, and Stewart remained standing.

'I will get right down to it. Nic is currently incarcerated on the suspicion that he is a spy. I assume you know of his previous connection to ASIO? In hindsight, it was not in his best interest to have his clearance upgraded, despite his best intentions to assist as an Air Marshall on the flight from Brisbane.'

The man paused for effect, and then a phone rang. He apologised for the interruption, moved over to his desk, and pulled it out from one of the drawers. Rose smiled as it was a bright red mobile phone, similar to the one she knew Nic had given to the South Australian Commissioner of Police during one of their first investigations. They had been teasing Nic that a Police Commissioner should have a red 'bat' phone as a tribute to the 'campy' Batman TV show from the 1960s, so Nic had purchased it for him. It had been welcomed as a lighter moment to deal with the dark days of fighting crime, even in Adelaide, South Australia. Stewart completed the call and rested the phone on the desk.

Rose nodded towards it. 'Well, Mr Stewart Humphrey.....you are actually the Australian Ambassador for the Consulate-General here in Dubai, aren't you?'

'Guilty as charged. We heard about Nic's gift to Commissioner Steldons in Adelaide, and I received one a couple of months ago. It's true about keeping things a bit lighter around here, especially when we explain the red phone connection to the original 'Batman TV' show to those that only know the more recent Hollywood versions.'

Gabriel nodded. 'The original is always best. Why did they ever bother to mess with the taste of Coca-Cola?' His comment eased the tension a little, and the man continued: 'The call I've just had confirmed Nic is being well looked after, and I have arranged to visit him if you are available. We can see him at four thirty this afternoon as there is a concert happening at the jail. Today is the birthday of one of the princes from the Dubai Royal Family. They have set it up for the prisoner's entertainment during their detainment.'

Xanthe and Gabriel shook their heads. 'Sorry, we've booked a trip on a Dhow cruise later this morning, followed by a tour at the Souk Markets, so we cannot attend. Thank you for the offer, though.'

Rose looked at Sandy. 'Thank you, Mr Humphrey; we would like to as long as we are not in the way.'

The man nodded. 'I will have my driver take you back to your Hotel as you need to change into something more appropriate. You must wear sleeves, jackets, and pants. Everything is air-conditioned, so you should not be uncomfortable.' He led them outside, and they declined his offer for transport again, climbed into the Goodenough's Hummer instead, and returned Rose and Sandy to their Hotel.

Xanthe and Gabriel had decided to reschedule their Souk Tour as the temperature was now pushing 45° in the shade, so Gabriel insisted the group head to the Mall of the Emirates for another shopping expedition. At least it was cool inside but it is full of more shops.

After the shopping expedition, the group again returned to Rose and Sandy's Hotel and waited for Mr Humphrey's driver. A sleek black Mercedes drove up, the driver got out and opened the rear door so they could see the occupant. It was the South African man that they had seen before.

'Please get in. I will take you to see Mr Thorn.'

Rose stepped back. 'No, thank you. We will wait for Mr Humphrey.'

The man exited the car, and Gabriel walked up to find out what was happening. Rose had mentioned that they'd been approached previously by a man purporting to be from the South African Consulate. Gabriel leaned towards the man and smiled. 'Unakuwaje.' The occupant looked at him.

'Nikusaidi vipi?' Gabriel offered instead, but the man continued to stare at Gabriel. 'I do not speak Swahili, Dr Goodenough.'

Gabriel continued. 'Then I will switch to English, Sir. Please leave, or I will call the Police.' The man shrugged his shoulders and handed Gabriel his Business Card, which Gabriel put into his trouser pocket without looking at it.

Meantime, the Hotel Security Officers moved towards the Mercedes. They led the driver back into the car and took his details down. The man climbed back in, and the car promptly drove off.

Sandy moved towards Gabriel. 'What was that all about?'

Gabriel shrugged. 'I don't know, but all I said was hello, and how can I help you?'

Sandy smiled. 'I thought 'Jambo' means hello in Swahili speak?'

'Sort of. Jambo is like saying 'G'day' in Aussie. I know the guy from somewhere, maybe he once sold me some shoes in the shopping mall.'

A white Toyota Land Cruiser drove up, and Mr Humphrey stepped out from the passenger side. 'What was it all about?' Gabriel again shrugged. 'Nothing, I think Xanthe and I will return to the Burj.'

Mr Humphrey nodded. 'Good idea, Dr Goodenough, but please don't intervene in matters of state here in Dubai. I know of our South African friend, and whilst he's a little confronting, he is relatively harmless.' Sandy and Rose stepped into Land Cruiser and they headed off to see Nic.

Stewart turned around to face Rose and Sandy. 'We are going to jail. It will be very confronting. Please avoid making eye contact with anyone. Do not speak unless you're spoken to, and please remember we are all guests. Oh, and don't laugh at whatever Nic is doing.'

The trip took over two hours, and they were now stopped at the entry gates. He turned back to them once again. 'Have either of you been in jail before?'

Rose and Sandy shook their heads. 'Well, this is a relatively new jail, so the conditions are much better than most others in the UAE. There are bad people in here. Please be careful, listen to my instructions and always keep safe. Have either of you used a gun?'

Sandy looked at him. 'I shot someone with a Taser Gun once.'

Rose shook her head. 'I was once bailed up by a broom-wielding bandit. It looked like a gun.'

Humphrey nodded and continued. 'Well, the viewing room is well away from the prisoners, so we shouldn't have to worry about being seen, but we have to keep safe at all times.'

Sandy nodded. 'Will we be getting 'Harry Potter 'cloaks of invisibility just in case? Nic once told Rose they are a real thing.'

He laughed. 'No, not quite. We'll be behind one-way glass.'

They were directed to drive through the double-height security doors and waited for the guards to assist them in exiting the vehicle. Their group was then escorted to a foyer and into an elevator. It took them two storeys high, and they stepped out to a windowed corridor.

Below them was a room filled with two hundred seated prisoners and about twenty-five heavily armed guards, and a large wooden makeshift stage was at the front. Music started playing and the crowd started clapping. The sound made its way into the room where Rose, Sandy and Stewart were watching.

The first artist was dressed entirely in black, had a black Stetson pulled tightly over his bowed head, and a guitar over his shoulder. He stood at the microphone. *'Hello, I'm Johnny Crash.'* The backup band started playing 'Folsom Prison Blues', the Johnny Cash classic.

It was Nic, and he led the band into the song.

Sandy and Rose enjoyed the show, and even Stewart managed to smile. 'Nic is quite good, isn't he? I didn't think he'd find trouble here in this place.'

The band wound up the song, so Nic grabbed the Stetson from his head, threw it to the floor, roughed up his dark, wavy hair with the other hand, and then pushed out the microphone on its base axis. He had taken the classic Elvis Presley stance. This time, the band started up with 'Jailhouse Rock.'

The audience enjoyed the show and some guards did Elvis 'hip-wiggles'.

Rose smiled. 'Yes, he finally has his audience captured and captivated.'

The second song finished, so Nic moved off the stage, and Stewart watched him leave. 'Please wait here. I'm off to find Nic and discuss his next decision with him. I'll let the guard know if the plan changes. He is part of my personal protection team and is carrying if needed.'

Sandy looked the guard up and down. 'Are you carrying a gun? Or did he say that to keep us on edge?' Stewart nodded. 'He's armed with a sharp wit and a small gun and trained in origami.'

Rose sighed. 'That's paper folding.'

'Yes indeed, as folding napkins are his forte.'

Sandy shrugged. 'Are you just trying to make us feel more comfortable, or do you think we have missed Nic's silliness.'

Stewart smiled, moved out of the office, and left them alone.

The guard moved towards them. 'I can't do the paper folding stuff, but I am armed, just in case you're wondering. Mr Humphrey is great to work for, but I think he's missing Australia, at least the inane Aussie humour.'

The three of them kept watching the show below from their secure room, and a group of men went up onto the stage. They were all carrying white laundry bags and proceeded to step inside them. A singer approached them, tied them off over their heads, and went up the microphone. The band started playing the John Lennon song, 'Give Peace a Chance'.

The guard smiled. 'It's 'bagism'. A tribute to John and Yoko. She once spent the whole time on stage in a bag when John performed, but here they'll probably get into trouble for dirtying the laundry bags.'

The crowd of prisoners below was now rowdy, and their guard was nervous. A phone on the wall then rang, and he answered it. 'Yes, thank you. I will bring them down now.' He looked at Rose and Sandy: 'Mr Thorn has been released into Stewart's custody, so we are good to go? We'll return to Stewart's house, not to the Embassy. We're having an Aussie barbeque for dinner, with prawns, snags, and everything salady.'

9

Their little group took the elevator back down to the ground, exited the jail and climbed back into the Land cruiser. Nic was sitting in the middle, so Rose and Sandy sat either side. He was still handcuffed but had a wry smile.

'Hey, I'm out of jail. Didn't have to pass GO or pay two hundred dollars.' Rose then noticed his left forearm was bandaged, but didn't comment.

After a drive of about two hours, they returned to Stewart's home. Xanthe and Gabriel were already there, along with a horde of eight children, ranging from late teens to newborn triplets.

Stewart stepped out of the vehicle, greeted his children, and looked back to the others who had climbed out of the car. 'Yes, they are all mine'. He then broke into song. 'Give me a home among the gum trees, lots of Humphreys, a dog or two, and a barbeque…"

Nic laughed. 'They're not words from the song, mate, but it is an Aussie classic. Can you get me out of these now, please?' He held up his hands as they were still handcuffed.

Stewart shook his head. 'Not until you're inside.'

The group moved into the house and Nic was released from the metal bracelets, and introductions were made: 'This is my wife, Gloria, and as for my children, I have no idea what their names are. There's too many of them.' He laughed at his joke.

Gloria welcomed the guests, cool drinks were offered all around, and they were directed to an enormous lounge room. The meal was served, and the servants plied them with the food. Dessert was now being cleared from the table, and the conversation eventually moved around to Nic's recent unwelcome interest in the Dubai government.

Stewart took control of the conversation. 'So Nic, I've given you a few days here in Dubai before you return. It will give you time to see the sights, get sand between your toes, and make goo-goo eyes with a couple of camels. Are you OK with that?'

'Sure. I've got to get to the top of the Burj anyway. It's on my bucket list.'

Rose looked at him. 'What else is on it?'

'Swimming with the whale sharks off Broome in Western Australia, the bull sharks in South Africa, and the loan sharks in New York City.'

'You dope.' Rose then looked to their host. 'Are we free to move around Dubai?'

'Yes, but please stay with the crowds and try to keep together.' He then handed them each a pager about the size of a thumb drive and had a red button on the top of the unit. 'Please use these if you need to get in touch with me.'

Nic's group bade farewell and returned to their Hotels. Rose and Sandy had to wait for Nic to collect a Christmas parcel from the front desk. It was addressed to 'Ken Obi'; so they assumed it was from Chewy in Australia.

They moved to the bar area, and Nic opened the gift. It was a replacement watch, and this time, it came with a wristband, so he attached it to his right forearm as his left one still bore the scars from the removal of the last one.

Rose looked at him. 'I thought you were Batman.'

Nic nodded. 'Yep, me too, but don't tell anyone as I'm also Obi-Wan Kenobi.'

They dined and then retired early to their rooms.

As Xanthe and Gabriel were staying at the Burj Khalifa, they were able access the view from the observation deck on the one-hundred-and-forty-eighth floor. They were waiting their turn in the queue for the lifts, and another ten tourists joined them to be ushered into the lift. During the ascent, a trio of locals had manoeuvred their way in front of Xanthe, and she was now separated from Gabriel within the small space.

The lift arrived at the designated floor, and the occupants moved out, however, Xanthe being barricaded, was not able to exit with them. One of the men stepped forward and pressed the button for the one hundred and sixtieth floor.

Xanthe tried to move forward. 'Excuse me. I need to get off.'

The men ignored her.

Meanwhile, Gabriel had turned around, and the last thing he saw was the escalator doors closing and concern on Xanthe's face. He remembered the pagers then realised he had both in his backpack, so he called Nic.

'Hi Gabriel, what's up? Apart from the escalators in the Burj?'

'I've just watched Xanthe being restrained. They stopped her from getting out of the lift with me. We were supposed to have got out on the observation deck, the highest one, but three ugly dudes didn't let her. The lift stopped on the one hundred and sixtieth floor. I think she might have been kidnapped.'

'Does she have a pager?'

'Nope, I've got both of them.'

'Give us fifteen minutes. We're next door in The Dubai Mall.'

Nic disconnected and looked over to Rose and Sandy. 'Let's go. Xanthe's could be in trouble.'

They started to run towards the nearest Burj Khalifa exit, and as they moved outside into the humidity the heat of the afternoon sun hit them.

'Guys, I think we'd better stop running.'

'Why? What have you seen?'

'Nothing yet. It's just too hot. Besides, we don't know what this is yet, and only mad dogs and Englishmen go out in the midday sun.'

Rose had slowed to a walk and took a swig from her water bottle. 'That's from a Noel Coward song.'

Nic caught his breath. 'Yep, and cowards don't run in the sun either; they just write songs about it.'

They moved towards the building and made their way inside.

Rose took a sip of water. 'So what do we do now, then?'

'Let's buy the tickets for the observation deck and hopefully save Xanthe from whatever she has got herself into this time.'

Rose looked at him. 'What's with 'this time? Just what has she done before?'

'Um, the last time I had to help her out was ....um.....' He was about to continue when Gabriel bounded up to them. 'I can't go any higher than the observation deck. They won't tell me who or what is up there, either. It's something to do with guest privacy. I wasn't going to explain to them why I needed to get up there.'

Rose looked at him. 'Did you try taking the stairs?'

'We can't get access?'

Nic looked at him, then waved his watch. 'Swoosh, swoosh. Do or do not; there is no try.'

Sandy looked at him. 'That's a quote from Yoda; I thought you were Obi-Wan?'

'I know; it's no wonder I'm confused. To the bat pole then, guys, but the escalator will probably work much better.'

The group ventured back into the building, purchased the tickets for the observation deck, stepped into the lift and rode to the one hundred and fortieth-eighth floor. They exited and looked for the stairs to access higher floors. Sandy returned. 'I've found it, but we'll need a pass card to get through the door.' They moved around to the area and contemplated their next move.

Meanwhile, Rose had collected a brochure on the building, flicked through it, and reached the final few pages. 'I know what's on the hundred and sixtieth floor. It's a mosque, but the building owners say that's a myth.'

Nic smiled, crossed himself and walked up to the panel on the door jamb. 'Bless me, Father, for I am about to sin.' The door clicked open, and he stepped through and held the door for the others to follow him. They were now in the stairwell and Gabriel looked at the closed door.

'Should we push the panic button and get Mr Humphrey involved?'

Nic shook his head. 'Not yet. We don't know what this is. It could be something harmless, and they could just be showing her the sights. They would not often get Agnetha from ABBA, here in Dubai.'

While waiting at the door, two young men with large backpacks moved past them and began ascending the stairs. Nic started to follow the young men. 'Go back to Gabriel's room and wait for me there. I'm going for a walk.'

Rose, Sandy and Gabriel returned to Gabriel's hotel room. It was only on the 38th floor, but still impressive, nonetheless. Sandy looked at the view, then back at Gabriel. 'I think something must be happening below as Television Vans are starting to gather, and people are setting up cameras. Maybe a Prince is visiting the building.'

'I'll call down to reception to see what it is.'

Gabriel made the call and came back a moment later. 'The two guys that passed us by the stairs are doing a BASE jump from the top. The last one was done about six years ago, so they want to try again and have built a platform on the hundred and six-tieth floor.'

Rose looked at him. 'That's where Xanthe is.'

'Yes, and I assume Nic is there too. I hope he's not thinking of jumping as there are only two parachutes. Let's go down to the ground and watch.'

They returned to the ground and milled around with the crowd, waiting for the show to start. Rose went off to ask the nearest security guard what and when it was all to happen and returned.

'The two guys have done it before. The jump takes about a minute. They'll open their parachutes and land in the water during one of the fountain displays. It's due to start in about two minutes.'

The gathering crowd was now numbering in the hundreds, and as everyone waited, Rose overheard someone say that the jumpers were outside and on the platform.

Gabriel took a deep breath and looked over towards the ground floor opening of the Burj Khalifa foyer and saw Xanthe being escorted from the building by two men. One had a gun slung from his shoulder. He nodded and whispered to Rose. 'I guess Nic didn't save her after all.' The second man prodded Xanthe in the back and propelled her forward.

In the meantime, the crowd watched in anticipation as the jumpers had leapt from the platform and began their descent. Gabriel sighed. 'What shall we do?'

Rose shrugged. 'Nothing. Let's watch the show and hope for a miracle.'

They watched as the two men and Xanthe headed in the other direction, away from them, away from the gathered crowd, and away from the safety in numbers.

In the meantime, the jumpers had opened their chutes, were doing circles to slow their descent and nearing the apex of the water fountain display. The two men with Xanthe were oblivious to the incoming jumper, and suddenly, one of the jumpers gathered an updraft, peeled off and headed towards Xanthe and the armed men. He lined them up, raised his legs and collided with the duo, pushing both gunmen into the water pool. Xanthe was now standing there all alone.

The first jumper, 'skated' across the top of the pond, made it to the edge and stepped onto the promenade. He unclipped his harness, removed his helmet, straightened his collar, and nonchalantly stepped into the crowd as if nothing had happened.

It was then Rose realised the second jumper was Nic.

They ran up to him, and Xanthe moved towards their group. The crowd started clapping and cheering. Nic started unclipping his parachute and looked towards the two men floundering in the water being attended by the Police. Nic shrugged. 'I guess I got the jump on them, didn't I?'

About an hour later, they had been collected by Mr Humphrey's driver and were at the embassy being served drinks. Gabriel suddenly stood up, removed a Business Card from his pocket and held it at his fingertips. 'I've got a massive apology to make here. I know who the South African man is.' He read the name from the Business Card: *Herschel Van Der Vaargen. Diamond Merchant.*

Xanthe was the first one to realise the significance of his confession. 'Herschel was supposed to be helping us track the origin of the diamond ring. We found his name on one of the emails to and from the TV station that awarded us with the diamond ring as a prize. We're so sorry.'

Stewart acknowledged his understanding of the situation. 'I was wondering who the link in all of this was. I've since found out he's been running a fake diamond scam out of Dubai. They're called Lab-Diamonds, created in a factory but sold as genuine. Only a gemologist, using spectroscopy to view fluorescence patterns, can tell the difference. We've been thinking it was originating in Dubai somewhere.'

The group moved into the dining room, and Gloria closed the door behind her. 'Herschel's two children attend the same school as our eldest girls.

Our Aggie had mentioned that he'd been helping a couple from Australia trace the origin of diamonds from Botswana. So, that's where it all started, then? That was months ago, though; I didn't realise you were here to track that down?'

Rose responded first. 'No, we're supposed to be on holiday, then we were heading to Africa to check it out. I guess, it wouldn't be in our best interests to continue, sorry, Xanthe.'

Nic sighed. 'Yep. Perhaps I needed a distraction from all the scams and things I've been looking and maybe I let my guard down.' Nic shuddered and shook. 'Aaaagh, I am Nic Thorn, a man among men, the man's man, and a man about town.' Then he struck the classic 'Superman' pose.

Rose looked at him. 'Are you quite finished, Cluck Kent?'

There was a knock at the door, more drinks were brought in and the room went quiet. Stewart moved towards Nic and whispered. 'So where to from here? You are still being deported from Dubai, but if I can keep this out of the online news feeds, are you happy to leave ASAP and return to Australia?'

'Aye, Aye, Commissioner Gordon.'

Rose shook her head at him. 'I'm confused. Are you now Superman or Batman? Even so, when did you learn how to BASE jump?'

'I didn't learn. You jump off buildings and start praying. There's nothing to it.'

Xanthe moved over to him and gave him a hug. 'But how did you know it was me down there?'

'Well, when I stepped from the stairs at the exit door, I saw Herschel and his goons wrestling to get the diamond ring from you. I overheard them saying how stupid they were to let the shipment of lab diamonds get into Australia. It was the third guy's fault, as they said something about him enjoying his last meal. When they talked about serving you a last meal, I thought I'd better do something. You could say I jumped to a conclusion.'

Rose shook her head. 'We'd never say that.'

'Anyway, we'd better return home. I may have to sit in cattle class to maintain a low profile, given that I'm an expelled tourist. How about you two, Xanthe? What are you guys going to do?'

Xanthe nodded. 'Gabriel and I will re-direct our tickets to Johannesburg instead of Nairobi. He's always wanted to show me around his hometown, then we'll head up to Namibia. There's a group of doctors that he'd like to catch up with.'

Within two hours, Nic, Rose and Sandy had returned to the Dubai Airport and were waiting to board the plane back to Australia. During the flight, Sandy and Rose searched for Nic and eventually found him in one of the last rows of seats at the plane's rear. He was alone, had three seats, and was sound asleep, softly snoring.

'Oh, isn't that sweet? The poor little tyke is pooped out.'

'Hey, I heard that, Rose. So, you found me, and I need another favour.'

They looked at him and waited to hear the details of their subsequent investigation. 'Not in here, guys. Please return to your Business Class plush seats, three-course meals, and soft pillows. Leave me here slumming in cattle class, and I'll catch up with you in a couple of days back in Brisbane.'

Rose sat down next to him, and Sandy remained standing. 'It's a long flight back, Nic, so before we go, will you explain what happened in Dubai and with the diamond?'

Nic leaned close to her. 'Let's just say some days are diamonds and some are stones. In this case, the diamond in the rough turned out to be a guy with some diamond connections.'

'But Mr Humphrey was the Consulate General, not a diamond dealer.'

'Yep, and he's on our side. He's arranged to replace the diamond ring. So when Xanthe and Gabriel return to Australia, she'll be wearing a real diamond from Dubai. I don't think she'll be disappointed.'

Rose looked at him. 'You mean we had access to a genuine diamond merchant that could get a high-quality stone for next to nothing?'

Nic grinned. 'Yes, Rose, but I had no idea you were looking to get married again.'

Rose shook her head. 'Damn you, Nic.'

10

Nic rang their front doorbell four days later, and Rose opened it. He stood there smiling and had a suitcase with hand luggage slung over one shoulder. 'Hi, Rose. I'm taking some time off, so would you mind taking me to the airport?'

'What's the new gig then? Are you going solo?'

'Well, no, and yes. No work, no stress, no fixing a scamming mess. Just me and my shadow sitting on a beach somewhere for a month.'

Sandy came up to join them. 'What's this about, going solo?'

Nic broke into the first verse of ABBA's Money, Money, Money song. *'I work all night, I work all day to pay the bills I have to pay...'*

Rose waited for him to finish, then added. 'That's not good.'

Nic looked at her. 'Rose, the line is *'that's too bad.'*

'I know the song, but I'm not joining your singing sessions. It's too early, and your warbling will wake up all dogs in the neighbourhood.'

They went through the house and onto the rear deck, where Dog was curled up in a Papasan, his fur and fluff spilled over the sides. Goliath was on guard in case of any unwanted interruptions.

Nic then noticed a Dachshund, guarding the top of the stairs and looked at the menagerie. 'I thought you guys might need a break from all the secret squirrel stuff, and it must be making you both all a bit squirrelly. I fly out in about three hours, but there's no hurry. I want to be there in about two hours, or we can leave now, and I'll shout you access to the Qantas Lounge. I'll reserve a room and explain what's happening.'

They decided to leave straight away for the airport and left the animals to guard the house. Sandy was driving, Nic was in the back seat and Rose turned around to face him. 'What happened to your watch in Dubai? And what's with that bandana tied around your wrist? Are you supposed to be disguised as Captain Jack Sparrow or a Pirate?'

He waved the bandana at her. 'Well, the watch is gone, and the bandanna covers the scar where they cut the tracker out. It makes me look cool and means I always have a handkerchief or a napkin handy to wipe my brow. I had to swallow the watch; it tasted like one of those Listerine flakes.

That was the agreement with Chewy, so it couldn't be taken from me and fall into the wrong hands. The technology is cutting-edge, using palladium circuitry and all that. When the Dubai dudes found the locator embedded in my forearm, they cut it out and were even nice about it. They even gave me a lovely leather belt to bite while extracting it.'

Rose nodded. 'It's tiny technology, so they would have to be tiny wrong hands. Are you getting another one sent from Melbourne? We need to keep track of your whereabouts, you know.'

'Nup, not enough time, so you might have to go old school. Just ring me occasionally instead.'

They parked the car and went to the room reserved in the Qantas Lounge. 'OK, take a big breath, guys.' Nic paused for effect. 'I'm finally cashing in all those accrued Qantas Loyalty points when you've been using my Credit Cards. I deserve a holiday, maybe you guys do too, but my points can only go so far.'

They looked at him, and Rose sighed. 'So, is this the end for Nic Thorn and Associates?'

'Not at all. I'm just taking a month off. Nic Thorn needs some Nic Thorn time.' Rose shook her head. 'Please don't do that.'

'What's that, Rose? Take time off?'

'No, talk in the third person.'

Nic grinned. 'The Aged Care thing will wait for us. Did you get a chance to read any of the financial reports, Sandy?'

'Nope, I was too busy wondering what scam investigation you were going to spring on us next, and to tell you the truth, I forgot about it, seeing that you were offering to take us overseas.'

Nic nodded. 'But you spent nearly thirty hours sitting in a plane with nothing to do but watch movies and eat.'

Sandy shook her head. 'That's not true, Nic. I had lots of sleeping to catch up on, but I have time to read it now.'

'Fair enough. I'm heading down to Sydney to catch up with my sister. Then, we're heading off on a month's family holiday. Destination unknown. I've left it up to them. I hope it's someplace with lots of golden sand and blue crystal water.'

Rose grinned. 'Maybe not Dubai then?'

'That's funny, Rose. I am allowed to travel overseas, but not as an ASIO spy, so I tell them I'm a member of the secret Australian Society Into Origami.

Rose shook her head again. 'Can we still get in touch if needed?'

'Yep, but there might be a time difference. We'll work it out, and if anything important comes up, you can get Chewy to deal with it. He has your numbers.'

'Just you, your shadow, and your Sydney sister, then?'

Nic shook his head. 'And the other one from Murrayville, and my folks.'

Rose looked at him. 'Make sure you take plenty of holiday snaps. We'd love to see what they look like.'

'That won't work, I'm still not letting you guys know what my family looks like. Ongoing family protection and all that.'

'Damn you, Nic.'

The flight was announced, and they watched him walk down the gangway. Sandy smiled. 'I bet you twenty dollars he doesn't look back.'

Rose nodded. 'You're on.'

About halfway down, Nic stopped, turned, looked at them, and returned up the gangway. They wondered what was happening, and as he came closer, he beckoned them to come forward, so they did, and he looked at them both. 'Guys, thanks for everything you do or don't do for me or with me, or nothing at all, as the case may be. You chose.' He turned back around, and they watched him leave. Again.

Rose looked over at Sandy and handed over the money. 'So, what do we do now for entertainment?'

Sandy grinned. 'Well, you heard what he said, we deserve a holiday too, and we still have access to his Business Credit Cards. I've heard about week stays at the Mooloolaba Radisson on the Sunshine Coast. Are you up for it?'

They returned home to look up holiday venues on the Sunshine Coast and found a five-night, six-day package with flights and car hire for a reasonable price. Rose looked at the cost of the trip. 'I know it's only an hour or so drive up there, but this way, we don't use our car and get to drive a convertible for the week.'

They went next door to tell their neighbour Dave they were heading off again, and the two little dogs followed them. Goliath was in the front, Dog in the middle and the dachshund trotting along behind. Dave was sitting in the front garden reading and looked up as they arrived.

'It looks like Dog's found another minion. I think the dachshund is from across the road somewhere, as some new people have moved in. Mum, dad and two kids. They're out all day, and the little guy must be getting bored.'

Rose chortled. 'Probably, so Dog has his two doggy-guards looking out for him.'

Dave nodded. 'It sure does. I think the little dude's name is Frank. I haven't met the owners yet, but I have seen the two dogs coming and going through their dog door and dragging out pieces of dog biscuits to present to Dog.'

'So we don't have to worry about keeping him fed then. Are you still OK if we go away again? Sorry, we keep asking you to do this.'

'It's all good, Rose. They follow me around on my morning walks, too. People come out to see the Dave and Dog Cat show, and I get to know the other neighbours. Where is Nic taking you this time?'

Rose shook her head. 'We're on our own for a month. He's taking a break. His sisters and parents are all going overseas somewhere and leaving us in charge.'

'Wow, getting on with your family as adults must be great. I have a sister in Darwin, but haven't seen or heard from her in years. I sometimes get a Christmas card. I suppose I should ring her.'

Rose nodded. 'Yes, you should. My brother and his wife used to live in Tasmania, then Nic organised for Eva to join a pro-golfing gig in Hawaii, and they live over there now. I still ring them.'

'Nic has a lot going on, doesn't he? Why did you come back so quickly from Africa?'

Sandy leaned down and patted Dog on the head, then to Goliath and Frank. 'We didn't get there. Nic was expelled from Dubai at the stopover, so we decided to come home. His friends, Xanthe and Gabriel, then went to Africa by themselves. Extended honeymoon, and all that.'

'I saw the pictures of their wedding online. They are a good-looking couple. I downloaded them to my iPad if you want to have a look. There are about five pictures, Nic and Sandy are in one. Rose, you, and the best man are in one too. He reminds me of a movie star, I can't remember which one, and she looks like the blonde from ABBA. Oh, to be that good-looking.'

Rose nodded. 'Nic told us that Chewy has a software program that removes any pictures of him posted online.' Dave headed off inside to get his iPad, and the women waited.

Suddenly, from across the road, a dog barked loudly. It was a large black mastiff, and the teenager holding the leash struggled to maintain control. The dog broke free from his grasp and rushed towards their little group. Dog hadn't moved and had his back to all the commotion. The two little dogs moved in front of Rose and Sandy and started barking in response to the intrusion. The charging dog stood in the middle of the road, bearing its teeth and being aggressive.

Sandy reached for Rose's hand for assurance, then they both looked down at Dog, he still hadn't turned around and assumed he was too busy with the catnip growing through the fence. Dave rushed out of his house, and the teenager was still frozen on the other side of the road. The din was getting worse, with all three dogs barking at each other.

Finally, Dog turned around to face the menacing threat, and the cat appeared to take a deep breath and then let out a defiant cry. 'Meeeowww!!'

The large dog stopped barking, looked at Dog, then at the other two little dogs, and the teenager finally moved over from the other side of the road to clip the leash onto the dog's collar.

'Wow, that was close. Lucky the big dog in the middle knew what to say.'

Rose looked at him. 'That's our cat. His name is Dog.'

'I'm sorry about that.'

'Are you sorry you thought our cat was a dog, or sorry that you lost control of your dog?' The lad shrugged. 'Um, I don't know. Brutus is not even my dog. It's my first day being a dog-walker, I'm not very good at it, am I?'

'Well, our cat just reminded your dog to behave itself in public and not to scare people.'

'Wow, Lady, can you understand cat-speak?'

'Yes, I studied it at the University of Kat-man-too, where you can study on-lion.' The young man nodded in agreement, and Dave shook his head at Rose's comments to the naïve youth. He then herded Dog, his two loyal companions, and Rose and Sandy through his front gate.

'Hey mate, how about you try looking after hamsters instead? At least they don't need walking around the block, just around the wheel.' The young man shrugged again, the mastiff took a big woof and then dragged the teenager away.

Dave pulled up the photos on the tablet, and they scanned through them. 'Huh? The one with Nic and Xanthe walking in is gone? I'm sure I downloaded them.'

'That's what Nic said would happen. His computer guy told us that he has a search and remove program that deletes any trace of Nic. It's a facial recognition thing.'

Dave grinned. 'Wow, Nic does have his secret squirrels working overtime on the treadmill. Anyhow, where are you heading off to?'

'Mooloolaba, on the Sunshine Coast. We pick up a flight, car hire and week stay, then we'll take an Uber to the airport at about eight tomorrow morning and return next Sunday afternoon.'

'OK, I've got to deliver Goliath back to my friend's place on Sunday night, so that will work.'

'Oh, we thought it was yours.'

'Nope. I wouldn't own a little dog like that. I'm a Border collie sort of guy, but they cost up to twelve hundred dollars, even more, if you buy them from a breeder with a champion lineage.'

Rose nodded. 'Good to know Dave, and thanks again.'

They returned home, and this time, only Dog followed them.

11

Rose and Sandy landed at the Sunshine Coast Airport, gathered the luggage, and arranged to collect the car. When they arrived at the Rental Desk, the receptionist welcomed them by presenting an upgrade, and it was to a Mercedes-Benz AMG GT E-Class. 'Thank you for choosing our Rental Service again, Miss Palmer. Mr Thorn has assured us that you would enjoy the upgrade.'

Sandy whispered to Rose. 'How did he know that we'd be here?'

'We used his Business Credit Card to book the holiday.'

'Damn you, Nic.'

'Hey, that's my line, Sandy.'

They went outside and found the car. It looked sleek, fast, and expensive, so they googled it. 'These cars are worth over three hundred and fifty grand. The insurance alone for the week will blow the budget, let alone Nic's mind when the bank statement arrives. I don't think I can do it.'

Rose nodded. 'You're right. Let's decline the up-grade and use the BMW Z3 convertible.'

They returned to the Car Hire booth and handed over the keys. 'Sorry we can't take this car, but thank you for the offer. Is there something a little less ...everything that's available?'

'Sure, Miss Palmer, but the BMW convertible is already taken. We do have a Chrysler PT Convertible. It's got silver door buttons for an extra bit of bling.'

'Thanks, we'll take that.'

Rose and Sandy located the replacement car, were shown how to use the fold-back roof and other features, and headed off to the Hotel. The accommodation was in the heart of the Mooloolaba Beach precinct, and the suite included three bedrooms, each with its deck with an un-spoiled view out to the bay from the 11th floor.

'Good choice, but why the third bedroom? Are you expecting someone else?'

'Nope, but Nic said he was going someplace with lots of golden sand and blue crystal water. This view foots the bill from what I can see, maybe he'll turn up here unannounced.'

'I don't think so, he's headed off overseas without us. Hey, I'm getting hungry, so can we eat now?'

They made their way down the street and walked through the myriad of restaurants along the foreshore, eventually settling on a place called

'Augellos – The World's Best Pizzeria.' They sat at a table set for four, ordered the meals, and enjoyed the casual ambience.

A couple of young girls came skipping along the paved promenade. The girls were giggling and oblivious to the waiter staff bringing the meals from the kitchen across the path to the alfresco tables. Some of the other diners had realised there was a blind corner, and everyone watched as the girls kept coming. None offered to intervene. A waiter carrying a pizza tray in each hand was about to emerge from Augello's kitchen. He hadn't yet seen the girls either.

Rose had seen them and began to stand, then nodded to Sandy. 'I hope that's not our pizza. Any moment it's going to end up on the ground.'

The waiter finally noticed the girls, but it was too late as they barrelled into him and he dropped the pizzas on the ground. The tray landed face down with a sodden plop. A couple of untethered dogs were passing and took their opportunity for the free lunch.

The waiter stood there looking at the mess on the path and watched the two young girls move away, and they hadn't even stopped to apologise. He approached Rose and Sandy. 'I'm so sorry, I didn't see them coming. It will only take twenty minutes to make another one, or we can offer you something else.'

Sandy responded. 'That's fine, just re-do the order. We're on holiday.'

Rose continued to watch the two young girls. 'I wonder where the parents are, Sandy.'

It was then she realised who they were. 'Oh, crap, this lunch just got a whole lot worse. Those two girls are Lucy and Skye. They're Michael and Dimond's children.'

Suddenly, there was movement at their table, as a passing woman had just pulled out a chair and sat down with them. It was Dimond.

'Hi ladies, fancy seeing you here. Have you seen my daughters? I think they went back to the Hotel without telling me.'

Rose nodded to the half-eaten mushed pizza mess on the footpath. 'Yes, they just breezed through, left their mark over there and skipped away.'

A flock of very happy seagulls were now cleaning up the residue. 'You might want to pay for that.'

'Did my girls do that?'

'Yes, Dimond, and they didn't hang around to apologise.'

'That's good, Michael has taught them well. He says it's always easier to ask for forgiveness rather than permission.'

'That doesn't make sense, Dimond. They should have waited for you and apologised to the waiter.'

Dimond nodded. 'Children, aren't they just wonderful? Anyhow, what are you guys doing here? And where is that handsome sidekick of yours, Nic Thorn?'

Rose sighed. 'We're on holiday, and Nic is off somewhere with his sisters and parents. We have no idea, but he'll let us know in due time. What about Michael? Is he here with you?'

'Nope. Too much work makes him dull. Hang on, maybe too much waiting for him to come home makes me dull too. Maybe that's why he works long hours and is never home. He's still in Brisbane, but now that you're here, I need your help. I've done something stupid.'

They both looked at her.

'All right, marrying Michael on the rebound from Rose may have been the first thing I did that was stupid, but he's a good man who loves his children. Besides, marrying him wasn't my fault; I was introduced to him on your wedding day.'

Rose shook her head. 'I didn't know you were there. It was over ten years ago. I was only nineteen when we married, so you would have been about seventeen. Why were you there?'

'His parents invited me as his younger brother's escort.'

'His brother would have been fifteen.'

'I know, weird, right? My parents said it would be OK, so I went to the show. It was my first time at a real wedding, and my second was to Michael a year and a half later. I often married Ken and Barbie, and it always worked out for them, so I thought it was that easy, and here I am, ten years and two children later. Oh, and it's my tenth wedding anniversary tomorrow.'

'Is Michael coming up from Brisbane to join you?'

'Oh no, he's too busy working. Getting duller by the day.'

Sandy was shaking her head, and the replacement pizzas arrived. They took a break from listening to Dimond as she'd finally stopped talking as she was eating their pizza. Her daughters had returned too, so she pulled over chairs for them.

As a kind gesture, the restaurant had made the larger sizes, so there was plenty round, but then the waiter recognised the two children and waited for an apology.

None was offered.

After about twenty minutes of uncomfortable silence, Rose and Sandy had only eaten half of one pizza between them, whereas Dimond and the children had finished the remainder.

Dimond finally spoke up. 'OK guys, so, I've ...um. Well, you know I've been looking to relocate across the Brisbane River to get closer to the girls' school. I've found some places to rent, and they haven't quite worked out as expected.'

Rose smiled. 'You lost out when the Real Estate Agents did a probity check on Michael and found he's on a high-risk list as a tenant?'

'It's nothing like that. I've been told both times that I was successful in getting the lease over the property, but when I returned a couple of weeks later, it all changed.'

Sandy shook her head. 'I don't get it.'

Dimond continued. 'Well, the first property was a five-bedroom home in Hamilton. The monthly rental was too good to be true. I met the guy who was renting the property, had a look, and handed over the three-and-a-half thousand bond in cash. He gave me a receipt and everything. I went back to have a look a week later and saw there was another family in there. I knocked on the door, and they told me they lived there. They'd been on holiday and had no idea someone had set it up as a rental.'

'Did you keep the receipt or anything?'

'Oh yes, I have it back in the Hotel Room if you want to see it.'

Rose shook her head. 'No, but don't tell us it happened again, then?'

'Well, the second time, a woman met me at a property in Clayfield. She said the property was her mother's, and the sale was going through a messy probate, so she was happy for someone to live in for a year or two while things got settled.'

Sandy nodded. 'So you handed over the cash for the bond and turned up a couple of weeks later, and people were living in it?'

'Oh no, I told her I would only put the money into a bank account this time, so I did. When I went back to this place, it wasn't there anymore. It had been demolished.'

'How much this time?'

'Four and a half thousand. It has six bedrooms and four bathrooms. The kitchen had been re-cently renovated too, so it never occurred to me it was dodgy.'

Rose sighed. 'This is why you need to use a Land Agent, Dimond, but what do you want us to do about it?'

'Well, I thought that with all the resources that Nic and his associates have access to, you should be able to find out something.'

'What happened about the bogus Bank Ac-count? Surely you could get the money back?'

'Well, no, Michael rang his Bank Manager, and they found out the bank account I'd put the money into was already closed. He also found out that the name on the account was someone deceased.'

Dimond took another piece of pizza. 'So will you help?'

'Nic is on holiday, but we'll run it past him. It might just be Nancy Drew and Miss Marple inves-tigating it, though.'

'OK, but what about you two? Not interested?'

'Yes, we'll do it too.'

'Great, there will be seven of us looking into it then, including Skye and Lucy.'

Rose shook her head. 'Sandy and I are heading to Australia Zoo this afternoon, so we're off to get changed. We'll phone you once we've spoken to Nic. It might take a couple of days to get in touch with him, though.'

'Great. So we'll see you there too.'

'Where? Surely you're not going to Australia Zoo today too?'

The children had overheard the conversation. 'Please, mummy, please take us.'

Dimond looked at her children. 'Sure, girls. Daddy said we can do anything you like when we are up here.' She then headed off with the children, leaving Rose and Sandy to apologise to the waiter for the children's previous antics and to settle the bill.

Rose and Sandy returned to the apartment to get changed, and both came out of their bedrooms dressed in bathing costumes.

Sandy looked at Rose. 'It looks like we're not going to the zoo at Beerwah then?'

Rose laughed. 'Nope, I've got a sudden urge to get some serious sun, and we need to check out the quality of the Surf Lifesavers here at Mooloolaba Beach.'

This time, they both laughed and headed for the beach.

The next day, they went to Australia Zoo.

12

They called Nic two days after spending time shopping at Sunshine Plaza in Maroochydore. The call was made via Zoom and the phone was on speaker. He answered, but there was no vision.

'This is Nic. If you don't want to leave a message, say, 'Nick off'. If you want to hold for someone else, please say, 'I don't want to hold Nic. If you want to hold for Nic, please say, 'I want to hold, Nic.'

'It's us, Nic. We know that you're there.'

'I thought you'd promised you wouldn't call unless it were an emergency. It's only been a few days.'

'It's been almost a week, Nic. It's not an emergency, but we want to run something past you. Have you heard of a scam where you pay a rental bond only to find out the property is already lived in?'

'Yep. It's an old one but a goodie. Have you guys fought, and Rose is moving out? You could live at my place, Rose. I would give you mate's rates.'

'I don't think so, You've got Ivy and the ugly troll that lives under your bed.'

'Good point. I forget so much now that I'm nearly fifty.'

'You're not even forty yet, Nic.'

'You're right, I forgot. So, what's up?'

Rose continued: 'It's Dimond. She's been scammed twice for the same rental bond thing. She's been trying to relocate the family across the Brisbane River and has handed over eight thousand dollars. Both times, the property rental offer was bogus.'

'Has she told Michael yet?'

'We think so.'

Sandy nodded in agreement. 'The first time she handed over cash, and the next time it was a bank transfer, but the account has since closed.'

'I'm not going to be able to do anything from here. Give Chewy a ring and get him to look into it.'

'So you're OK with us using him?'

'Of course, you guys are part of Nic Thorn and Associates, as much as he is.'

'Where are you, Nic?'

'I'll show you.' He turned on Zoom to 'view' and showed them around.

There was a beautiful beach with golden sand and blue crystal water, but as he turned the phone back around, they noticed a pair of long legs lying beside him on a beach lounge. The movement was too quick to catch who they belonged to.

'Damn you Nic, you're in Hawaii. It looks like you're out in front of the Outrigger Waikiki Beach Resort, and what's more, you have got company.'

'Good guess. I can't get anything past you, can I? Would you like to say hello to my sisters then?'

'Really?'

'Sure. I'm ....sorry....the signa....is ..breaking.....up.'

They assumed the call was terminated.

Rose continued. 'Damn you, Nic. If you can still hear us, that's nasty being over there without us.'

'I can still hear you, so I'll just have to say goodbye to all of them.'

Rose disconnected and called Chewy. It went to the message: 'Hi, you've called Chewy. If you want to hold for someone else, please say, 'I don't want to hold Chewy. If you want to hold for Chewy, please say, 'I want to hold Chewy.'

'Hi Chewy, it's us. Are you there?'

Chewy responded this time. 'Yes, my Angels.'

'Hey, that's Nic's line, and so is the other one about being on hold.'

'I know, I just wanted to try them out, but 'Chewy's Angels' doesn't quite work or the other one. It sounded funny when Nic did it. What's up?'

They updated him about Dimond's dilemma and the rental scam so Rose prompted him for a response.

'Is there much we can do, or should we just give it a miss?'

'There is enough for me to go on based on the name of the closed account, but you might have to get involved so we can set up a sting. Are you guys up to it? Nic is on holiday, so you won't have his backup. Oh, and are you going to charge her for our services?'

Rose nodded. 'Yes, we'll charge, so have an invoice ready or whatever you do, and we think we can handle the rest. Is there anything else we need to do?'

'Not yet. I'll get some ads posted online seeking high-end rental properties in the Clayfield and Hamilton areas of Brisbane, urgent, that sort of thing. Then, set you up as a couple of lawyers relocating from Melbourne, looking to find a property. I'll link it to a phone number to ring and will ring your numbers. It will appear with the name you are pretending to be.'

Sandy leaned forward. 'That sounds like a plan, but will it work?'

'It should do. It's a low-level scam. The people involved would not expect to be investigated, but it's unlikely that we'll get any money back. It's more likely the Police will stay out of it, too. We'll have to see what happens. I'll call you in a couple of days.'

They disconnected the call and Sandy looked at Rose 'So are you afraid of doing this on our own?'

'Not really. I'm more afraid of what names Chewy will use for us.'

After about an hour, their phones chimed as emails had been sent from Chewy. It showed the ad that he had posted:

Urgent Rental Property needed, please – Two Lawyers relocating from Victoria.

Clayfield, Hamilton, and Ascot area only.

Pay high $$$

Contact Heidi Cash or Breckin De Lore at De Lore Lawyers, Melbourne

Rose re-read the names 'I wonder if I'm Heidi or Breckin? Neither of us can do a man's voice.'

Sandy nodded. 'I've just googled it. It's a name that's neutral gender and also means 'freckled' in Welsh.'

Rose grinned. 'Beam me up, Spotty, and we'll wait to see what happens when a call comes through.' Sandy sighed. 'But how is the caller going to get in touch? There's isn't a number listed in the ad.'

They googled De Lore Lawyers, Melbourne, and it showed a high-end Legal Firm, referencing the business's longevity and clientele. There were a few other Lawyers' names and references.

'Wow. That was quick of Chewy to set all this up.'

Rose decided to ring him again. *'Hi, you've reached Chewy. I'm busy servicing the Millennium Falcon at the moment. Please leave a message.'*

The call ended with a guttural barking from the Star Wars movie by Chewbacca.

Sandy shook her head. 'That's not a very professional message, is it?'

'Nope, but we rang from my number, so it's probably just for us. Have you seen any of the Star Wars movies yet? A Movie Marathon is showing at the Sunshine Plaza Shopping Centre cinemas. Do you want to go there for dinner and a show? At least I can watch one of them; it may be the first one, which is apparently the fourth one.'

Sandy nodded. 'Sure, and we can keep hiding from Dimond for a while too.' They returned to the shopping centre, trying to keep a low profile and hopefully not run into Dimond and the children.

They found a park, had dinner at a restaurant in the shopping centre, and six hours later, returned to the apartment. Not having their phones on during the movie meant they were eager to see if there had been any response to the rental ad.

There wasn't, and they were disappointed.

They were sipping on Chardonnay, sitting on one of the apartment decks overlooking the ocean, trying to work out the next step. Rose sighed. 'It's only been half a day since the ads went online, but at least we have decent names this time. I don't know who I am yet though.'

Sandy nodded. 'I don't think it will matter, as the calls will come through from De Lore Lawyers, so we can pretend we are Executive Assistants again like we did in Adelaide. That time, you were Ringa-Rosie, and I was Sandy Olsson.'

Rose shook her head. 'I know, and now Nic has come up with the name Rosa Giardino for the Aged Care thing. I can cope with all of those names compared to the one I would have been stuck with if I was still married to Michael.'

'Remind me what his surname is again? I thought you would have kept yours anyway.'

'Oh no, he insisted that it had to be changed. I told him it was ridiculous, and that was our first fight. I think it was our second. Our first was that he wanted to kiss me at the wedding. I told him no way.'

'So what's his surname?'

'Bush.'

'You would have been Rose Bush, so that's even worse than you marrying Nic Thorn, and being Mrs Rose Thorn.'

'Yes, and it gets worse. I found out later that my Father fell for the stupid story Michael had been telling everyone in school, and that's why it was so important for me to marry him.'

'What was that one?'

Rose grimaced. 'Michael told everyone he was related to George W. and George H. Bush, the former Presidents of the United States.'

They laughed, and Rose's phone rang. It showed a re-direction from De Lore Lawyers, so she took the call. 'Welcome to De Lore Lawyers. Our office is currently closed. Please leave a message or call in the morning, and we will respond. Thank you.'

Rose quickly closed the phone and waited to see if a message was left. There was, so they listened to it: *Hello, this is Mark Wilson from Clayfield Real Estate in Brisbane. We have seen your ad and would happily assist you in relocating. I will call you back in the morning.*

'It's probably not the scammers, as that sounds like a legitimate business. My Father uses them, but I've never met that man.

Sandy nodded. 'But I don't understand how we're going to recognise the call is from a scammer'.

'I thought about that. If the calls are from legitimate agents it will generate a number and link straight into your contacts list. If it's a scammer, it will come up with "Call Barred" or "Caller ID unknown." That is what happens when Michael calls me.'

'So he still calls you then?'

'Yes, I could play you some pitiful messages he leaves. I delete them without listening to them.'

'How do you know he leaves a message?'

Rose sighed. 'He always rings back a few hours later to let me know. Maybe the next time he rings, I'll answer, tell him to nick off, and remind him that I'm with Nic Thorn now.'

'Are you with Nic Thorn?'

'No, I thought we both were. Besides, we made the pact; neither of us goes there.'

'Yes, it's weird. This is the longest relationship I've had with a man, nearly two years, yet it doesn't feel like it. I still recall meeting him at Uncle Albert's funeral and thought he was a bit over the top, but here we are two years later, still working with him. How is the Morgan restoration going? I saw it sitting outside the mechanic's business with a 'For Sale' sign, but there wasn't a contact number.'

Rose nodded. 'Yes, when a car sits near their shop, it sells quickly as they won't put their name on it if it isn't a good buy. I'm looking around at the moment for another car. It's probably another convertible, as they tend to flip easily. Men either want one when they go through a mid-life crisis, or they want to keep their wives happy now that they're empty nesters, or want a fun run-around to keep their wives happy to keep them out of the house.'

Sandy's phone rang, and they looked at the number. It was Nic.

'Hello, Angels. This is your Bat-man, and I have a riddle for you.'

Rose sighed. 'It's too late for pop-culture references, Nic. What's up?'

Nic continued: 'Nothing, just checking in. Did Chewy sort everything out? There's a twenty-hour difference between Brisbane and Hawaii, so I thought I'd call you tomorrow to check out what you did yesterday.'

'What's the time there now? It's getting near ten p.m. here.'

'It was six o'clock yesterday, or is it tomorrow? I'm not sure; are we there yet?'

'Nic, what do you want?'

'Nothing. I'm dining with my sisters tonight. We spent the day touring, and my folks have already headed off to bed, so I thought I call you guys to say 'Aloha.''

'Everything's fine here, and Rose is even going on a date.'

'Wow, that's a lot happening, anyway; just keep me updated via email until I get back.' They disconnected the call and looked at each other. 'He said nothing when I mentioned you're going on a date.'

The phone rang again. 'Yo, it's Nic again. Who's the date with Rose?'

'You don't know him.'

'Ah, but I can find out.'

'OK....he works for a Government Agency, and if I tell you anymore, he'll have to kill you.'

'Fair enough. Be careful and keep safe.'

'Thanks, *Dad.*'

There were not many other calls from Real Estate Agents by the time they were back home in Brisbane, and they were disappointed that their ploy may have been a waste of time.

Rose and Sandy were sitting on their rear deck, pondering their next move and Dog and Goliath were curled together in the Papasan. Suddenly, the cat raised his head, jumped off and was now at the top of the stairs, watching and waiting on something happening down below.

'Something's up, Rose. The last time Dog did that was when Michael arrived unannounced. I hope he's not here again. Otherwise, we might have to consider moving.' A voice called out from below.

'Hello, it's us, Michael, and the children. We're back from Maroochydore, and we have news.'

'Damn, it's Dimond. What are we going to tell her about our lack of success?'

'I don't know, Sandy, but we should let her up anyway. Can you go inside and give Chewy a ring to see if he's come up with anything.'

'I'll put the phone on speaker, so it sounds like we've got company.'

13

Sandy went inside, and Rose stood up to greet the visitors. Dog had now moved from the top of the stairs to halfway down, and Dimond and the girls went to move up the stairs, but Michael stayed well behind them. He had met the cat before and was unsure what it was capable of. It was an eight-kilogram beast, after all, whilst Michael was all of sixty kilograms, ringing wet.

'Mummy, is that a cat or a dog?'

'Skye, it is a cat, but Daddy is scared. So please don't embarrass him.'

'I don't think we could embarrass the cat, Mummy.'

'I was referring to your Father.'

Meanwhile, Goliath decided to make a move and went down the stairs. He couldn't get around Dog, so he walked over the top, reached the bottom of the stairs, looked at the children, gave a welcome woof and moved toward Michael. As the little dog approached him, it turned around to look at Dog as if he wanted permission to do something. The cat stopped washing and appeared to nod, then the little dog bit Michael on the leg and scampered off.

Dimond ignored Michael prancing about holding his ankle and called up to Rose. 'We've had another call from an agent. It sounded much like the same thing as before. Michael's here to talk about what we do next.'

'OK, come up and take a seat. We have someone else here, so Sandy will be out in a minute or two. I don't think Michael needs to come up. Can we offer you a drink?'

'No, thank you. I've given up drinking.'

Rose looked at her. 'All right. Michael told me to stop drinking wine around the children.'

'Really?'

'Yes, but I can. Have you got a gin and tonic? Michael's had said only to stop drinking wine.'

Sandy came back outside with a tumbler, two lemon cordials for the children and nothing for Michael as he was waiting below watching Dog. Dimond and her two girls had taken the stairs, gingerly stepping over Dog as the cat was lying across a single step. They reached the deck and sat down around the table.

Rose was waiting for the conversation to start but didn't, so raised the topic. 'So, did another call come through? We've got nothing from the work that we did. Chewy will send Michael an invoice for our efforts.'

'He'll sort that out. A message was left on our home phone. A property has become available at number nine Slade Street, in Wooloowin. Four bedrooms, three bathrooms, blah, blah. We've already done a drive-by, and a house is there.'

Sandy looked at her. 'Did you talk to the neighbours about it?'

'Not yet, but the caller wants to meet me on Sunday morning for a viewing at ten a.m. before they go to church.'

Rose looked at Dimond. 'Why do you think that's suspicious?'

'Who goes to church these days? The call must be from the scammers.'

Sandy shook her head. 'My Father goes to church, Dimond.'

'Doesn't he live in Adelaide? You know that is the city of churches. There's a pub on one corner and a church on the other, with a pastor in between selling the sacramental wines by the case full.'

Rose nodded. 'OK, but it still doesn't make sense.' Dimond continued: 'Oh, the caller did say I needed to make sure I brought along the rental deposit in cash.'

'All right, it makes sense then. Was there anything else left on the message?'

'Oh yes. The caller told me to come alone.'

Michael called out from below. 'Are you guys finished yet? Your cat is giving me the evil eye.'

Skye stood up and leaned over the deck. 'Not yet, Daddy, the kitty won't hurt you. It likes you.' Michael looked up to her. 'Why do you say that, Skye?'

The girl moved back to her mother and sat down. 'Well, Dog only told the little dog to give you a nip. If it didn't like you it would have told it to wee on your leg.'

Dimond gently patted Skye on her head. 'OK, Rose. Are you guys going to come along with me? We could be like Charlie's Angels, the Kung-Fu fighters. I loved Drew Barrymore in the film. What a great movie, so original.'

Rose shook her head. 'Not quite Dimond, it was a remake of the TV series from the late '70s. The original Charlie was in their remake, though, John Forsythe. He was also Blake Carrington in Dynasty. I've been watching the re-runs.'

'Thanks, but can we at least go in matching kick-ass outfits?'

'No. We'll be there, but keeping a low profile. We might go in disguises if we can get to Nic's warehouse at Bowen Hills between now and then.'

Dimond rubbed her hands together. 'Mr and Mrs Old people? Or something hip and pretty, like

Penny and Bernadette from that Big Bang TV show?'

Rose shook her head. 'We might need to be invisible. We worked with one of Nic's men on a caper in Adelaide, and he left his cloak of invisibility for us.'

Skye looked at her. 'Wow, it works, and Harry Potter is a wizard?'

'Yes, little lady. You never know what happens when you grow up. So, remember to be good to your mummy and daddy, and study hard at school.'

Skye crossed her hands across her chest. 'Please do not be patronising. I do not appreciate it.'

Sandy and Rose looked at her, and Dimond smiled. 'She's learnt that from me. I've used it on Michael, maybe a little too much? Children pick up so much from us, don't they?'

'We wouldn't know about that, Dimond.'

Dimond shrugged. 'Anyhow, what do you want us to do now, Rose?'

'Nothing, just go home, but expect us to be somewhere near the property at ten tomorrow morning.'

Dimond nodded to her girls, and they made their way back down the steps, gathered Michael and were on their way.

Sandy looked at Rose. 'Do we need to call Nic or Chewy if we're going to do some surveillance?

We'll need cameras, periscopes, and even one of those listening things. Maybe we could get Dimond to wear a wire and give her electric shocks if she talks too much.'

'Exactly what I thought, but not about the electric shock thing. Let's call Chewy.'

They dialled, put the phone on speaker, and he answered promptly. 'Hi, guys. I was just on the phone with the team in Bowen Hills. Let us put a surveillance kit together, just in case. It's ready if needed. What's up?'

'You must be psychic. Dimond has just left, and that's why we were ringing.'

'Yes, I'm Nic's psychic sidekick. The real Batman has Robin; Nic's got me.'

Rose leaned forward. 'Batman's not real, Chewy.'

'Wow, and yet they've made so many documentaries about him. I never knew and I thought everything you see on TV was real. It's just the stuff on the internet that's make-believe.'

Rose shook her head. 'Anyhow, so tell us about the spy stuff. Is it simple to use? We've only got until tomorrow to learn it all.'

'Nup, our guy will be with you and give you a rundown. The equipment is high-tech, so they'll need to operate it if needed. It's actually blurring the legal lines of the law, so we have to be careful.'

'When can we meet with them? Dimond's meeting at a property with the Land Agent at ten tomorrow.'

'I'll call now and send you a couple of websites to look at so you get an understanding of the equipment. Let's set it up for a meeting at eight tomorrow morning at the warehouse.'

Rose nodded. 'Sounds like a plan. What's his name?'

'Seiko.'

'Seiko, as in the Japanese watch brand?'

'Yes, our go-to surveillance guy. Cool name for someone that watches, isn't it?'

Rose sighed. 'I assume it's not a real name either. All part of Nic's secret squirrel stuff?'

'Something like that. Anyway, everything will be set for you to have a look at. It won't be used unless you think that Dimond needs to wear a wire. It's catching them after the event, not during it. There'll likely be a car chase, but don't get your hopes up.'

They hung up from Chewy and called Seiko at Bowen Hill warehouse. There was no answer, so they left a message introducing themselves, and an hour later, emails arrived with links to the surveillance equipment.

Bright and early, around 7 a.m., Rose and Sandy were waiting at the warehouse. The door clicked open, and they wandered in. A man's voice cried out from inside: 'Over here, Rose and Sandy.'

They moved to the sound, then another call from to their left. It was a woman's voice. 'Over here too.' They stopped, and Rose shook her head. 'We're not moving again until you show yourself.'

There was a sound from above, and someone in black combat fatigues dropped from the ceiling above and landed softly on the concrete just near them. A black balaclava was drawn from the head, revealing a young woman who looked a little like Dee-Dee, whom they had met before filming The Brain Haq.

Rose held out her hand. 'So Dee-Dee, are you Seiko too?'

'No. I'm her older sister. I'm Seiko. We both have quite a few things to do around here, but mostly, I get to play with toys that I can't afford to buy myself. Did you look at the websites and the equipment? Nothing will likely happen today anyway; we'll just be prepared. And yes, I like to watch data too, so it makes sense to cross-skill, doesn't it?' Seiko unclipped her harness and led them through the warehouse into a security area. The small room was full of wireless bugs, GPS trackers, audio jammers and directional listening devices.

'I've put a kit together, but we shouldn't need much. It's more about not getting caught yourself, rather than spying stuff and having to explain what you are doing with all the spying stuff.'

Rose nodded. 'Good to know, but we did think of something. Dimond said she was supposed to bring cash for the rental deposit. So, unless she's got bundles of it sitting around at home, I don't think she'll have it with her today.'

'Isn't her husband an Accountant?'

'He is.'

'Well, that generally means he'll have access to a safe and probably cash. They don't just hide money from the Government, but from everyone else too. That doesn't matter anyway, as I will provide the cash to hand over. We'll just have to get it to her.'

Sandy nodded. 'Marked bills? Is that what they call it? You've recorded all the serial numbers, that sort of thing?'

Seiko shook her head. 'Nope. It's micro-dotted; that serial number stuff and exploding dye packs are old school. I've got a scanner to run over the notes, and the dots get on the hands of anyone who touches the cash. When you think about it, it's gross how far the notes get into circulation.'

Rose nodded. 'Do you need us to do anything with the equipment? Are you going to be giving us lessons or anything?'

'I can show you what they do, but we'll likely be just sitting around watching, listening, and following. I'll get you guys to walk a couple of dogs, stop for a chat, that sort of thing, but you won't see me, as I'll be invisible.'

Sandy grinned. 'Gee, many of Nic's guys are good at being invisible. Did you all go to the same secret squirrel spy school or something?'

'Something like that. It's not that hard; you have to blend in. You wear your gym clothes if a fitness class is in a park. If you are walking a dog, make sure you have a dog. It's about practice and patience. I think our main concern will be Dimond. When Nic and Chewy told me about this scam, I started following her, watching and seeing how she reacted in different circumstances. She spends a lot of time drinking alone, but I would too if I married a guy like her husband.'

'You know that Rose married him about ten years ago.'

'Yes, Nic told me, and he told me about meeting Michael at Uncle Albert's funeral, too. You two have been good for Nic, more than you know. Just don't tell him I said that. We've still got about two hours before the party starts. Have you got Dimond's phone number or know where she lives? We have to drop the cash off.'

Rose shook her head. 'Nope to both. If I call, Michael might answer; if I visited, who knows what that will mean or where it will end up.'

'That's OK. I'll get Chewy to find it, then send her a text. She does spend a lot of time doing charity work, doesn't she?'

Sandy grinned. 'It's called penance.' Seiko laughed. 'It doesn't matter what it is, Sandy, but don't use any names from now on.'

Seiko's phone chirped ' OK, she's just responded and wants me to put the cash in a fishing tackle box and drop it into a boat parked in her driveway. Do you two want to come?'

Rose shook her head. 'Nope, we never want to know where she and Michael live.'

'Good point. OK, I'll see you at Wooloowin around ten. Here, take these.' Seiko handed them each an earplug. 'They're already blue-toothed to your phones. Just talk normally, and remember, if you answer your phone, just don't put it up to the ear that has the earplug in it. You might not hear from me, or see me anyway.'

Rose and Sandy returned home to West End and asked Dave if they could borrow Goliath. They knew the tea-cup dog wouldn't be big enough for a leash, so Sandy found a large handbag that would suit. They knew that Dog could handle a leash, so they took him for additional support.

The next issue was changing their car over to something less conspicuous as their only vehicle was decorated with "The She Shed." Seiko had arranged access to a Toyota Prius, and those cars are renowned for not having overly large seats. It was quite an effort to get Dog into the back seat, so they gave up and secured him in the front passenger seat. He sat upright with Rose in the back with Goliath, and Sandy drove. It was only about a twenty-minute drive across town.

14

It was just before 9:45 a.m., and the property at No. 9 was in the middle of the street. Sandy stopped at the top of the road, and their menagerie stepped out of the car. Dog took everything in his stride, and wasn't afraid of the unfamiliar surroundings.

They saw Dimond and her girls waiting at the front of the property but could not see Seiko. Rose and Sandy had brought along coffee-keep cups so they would appear to be doing a morning walk. Rose took hold of Dog's leash and rolled it through her hand to maintain control. She was concerned that it had been a while since he'd been on a lead. The cat looked up at her.

'I think Dog's got the leash thing worked out, Sandy. Are you good with Goliath?'

Sandy nodded.

They moved along the footpath, and a car pulled in close to them and parked. A man and woman were inside. They nodded towards Dimond, waiting further up the street, but only the man stepped out of the car. He had not seen Rose and Sandy, as his focus was on Dimond.

Rose whispered. 'I would say this is them. Let's stop and watch.'

Rose lightly pulled on the leash, and Dog promptly sat.

Sandy placed the handbag on the ground, and Goliath cautiously stepped out, then noticed Dog sitting there unfazed and tottled over to sit nearby.

Meanwhile, the woman had stepped out of the car. She was now leaning against it and lit a cigarette. She hadn't noticed the group behind her. Rose noticed that the rear registration plates on the car were missing, so she left Sandy holding Dog's leash and moved forward to check the front.

The smoking woman moved further along the road, providing enough room for Rose to look casually at the front. There was no plate there either; so Rose turned back to face Sandy, took out her phone and aimed it toward the VIN details on the windscreen.

'Hey, that's a great shot, Sweetie. Let me take your picture of you three standing there.'

The man, meantime, had reached Dimond and was twirling a set of house keys in his hand. They made small talk, and he gestured to her group to come inside to take a look. They were too far out of earshot for Rose and Sandy to overhear.

After about twenty minutes, Dimond and her girls came out again; they were smiling, and the man shook their hands. Sandy looked at Rose. 'I'm glad that didn't take long; I think Dog wants to take a look around himself, so let's get back to the car before he takes off.'

They moved back along the footpath and secured the animals.

The woman stubbed her cigarette into the ground as the man jogged up to her, and they drove away.

'So what now, Rose?'

'We wait. Seiko would have it under control. But you'd think that those two chumps would have said something to us; I mean, it's not every day you see a tea-cup dog standing next to an eight-kilogram Maine Coon cat in the middle of downtown Wooloowin.'

They watched the car go down the street, and it turned the corner; further along, a sleek black motorbike took off. It made the same turn.

'I'm going to get the cigarette butt, Sandy.'

Rose pulled out a plastic bag from her pocket, walked up to it, took a picture with her phone, picked it up with a small pair of tweezers and dropped it into the bag, then moved back to the car.

Sandy looked up. 'You can't collect evidence. We're not the police.'

'No, but Chewy said the police wouldn't be interested in this scam anyway. It's just in case.'

They were sitting there, and Rose's phone rang. It was Seiko and the sound of a motorbike engine came through her earpiece. 'We've followed them back to a Real Estate Agency in Clayfield. They've parked out the back. I didn't see if they took the money. Do you know if Dimond handed it over?'

'We're not sure. The man was wearing a coat and didn't have a briefcase. He might have put it into his pocket.'

'OK, I'll go inside the agency and see who they are. Hang on, I don't need to as their pictures are displayed here at the window. His name is Mark Wilson, and the woman is Renee Crown.'

'Wait there; we'll come to you. I'll call Dimond and get her to go there too.'

'Roger that.'

Sandy drove towards the agency, and Rose called Dimond. 'Hey, it's me. We've tracked them to an agency on Hamilton Road at Clayfield. Did you hand them over the money?'

'Yes. Three thousand dollars. It was enough to get the property, though.'

'There was five thousand in the envelope, Dimond.'

'Oh, I didn't know. Michael said he'd had a peek inside the envelope at home even though I'd told him not to. I'll meet you there.'

Rose and Sandy arrived, and Dimond was waiting out the front.

They left the two children in the car looking after the animals and entered the premises. Seiko was at the front of the group. 'Hello, my name is Seiko, and I'm looking for Mark Wilson and Renee Crown, as they're going to show me something.'

The receptionist smiled. 'I'm sorry, Miss, they're both in the conference room with a prospective client.'

Seiko responded quickly. 'Please go and find them, otherwise, we might start having a look around myself.'

The receptionist glared at them. 'Can you at least tell me what this is all about?'

Seiko became more abrupt with her. 'No, we won't.'

Rose then proceeded towards the nearest meeting room, and as the glass walls were opaque, she could only make out the silhouettes of two people sitting down and another one standing. Meantime, Sandy nodded to Dimond. 'Did you check out the faces in the window? Do you recognise anyone?'

'Yes, the woman was the one that showed me the demolished property, and the man that took the cash is there too.'

Rose nodded. 'So four people here are running a Real Estate scam out of a legitimate office. I think we may be out of our depth. Where's Nic when you need him?'

Rose rapped on the door, turned the doorknob, and stepped into the room. 'Excuse me; I am looking for Mark Wilson and Renee Crown. Are they in here?'

The man conducting the session was dressed in motorcycle leather, and Rose noticed a black helmet on the table next to him. He stopped talking and looked at her.

Rose stifled her smile as it was Nic.

He looked back at her. 'Hello, Miss. How can I help you? What is this all about…?'

Rose closed the door and returned to reception, where Seiko was making a phone call.

Meanwhile, Mark and Renee had left the conference room and returned to the office. 'How can we help you? There are four of you so that last property we just showed Dimond won't be big enough.'

Nic followed them out. 'Actually, it's probably somewhere smaller than you are all headed for. A lovely little prison cell with a lovely view overlooking the Wacol bush, with a metal front door too.' Mark turned to face the group. 'I'm sorry, but what are you talking about? And what was with the rude intrusion? Who are you?'

Seiko reached into her jacket pocket and then folded out a Police badge. 'Actually, it is Constable Seiko Russo and your little rental scam is over.'

Rose, Sandy and Dimond looked at her, and Dimond was the first to speak. 'Wow, a real cop so I might get all my money back after all.'

A car pulled up at the front door, and two people emerged.

Rose noticed them place a 'Police Business' on the car's front windshield. One had a small black rectangular box, and they entered the building. Seiko approached them, whispered something to the lead, and pointed to the chest.

The senior female officer took over. 'I'm Senior Detective Audrey Francis, and this is my partner Detective Myles Cook. We are holding you all on suspicion of fraud and deception. This office will now be closed pending our further investigations.'

Mark Wilson stepped forward. 'What evidence do you have?'

Nic grabbed his wrists, and Seiko held the scanner over his hands. It showed up the micro-dots. 'This.'

Seiko then grabbed Renee's wrists to carry the scanner over them. 'Oh, by the way, we have a search warrant and suggest your co-operation. I believe you have a safe here.'

The man reluctantly nodded and led them through the office to a safe. He opened it and inside were six envelopes. Each had different writing and dates and mainly were unopened. Dimond had followed them in.

'Hey, that one's mine. It's got our Xmas stickers on it. You'll see it's been signed across the seal at the back by Michael.'

The Detective turned it over, showing Michael's name and signature. 'Can I have it back, please?'

'Sorry, Ma'am, it's evidence. You will get it back eventually, though.'

Nic then directed his crew to the conference room for an explanation. 'I'm sorry guys, I came home early. I got bored and was missing all the excitement.'

The investigation ended after about an hour; initial statements were taken, and the perpetrators were allowed to leave. They were directed not to leave the state as formal charges would be laid later.

Rose was standing on the street with Nic. 'Did you hear Dimond say that only three thousand were in the envelope?'

'Yep, so two thousand dollars is missing. It doesn't matter though, as it was covered in microdots, so anyone trying to use the notes will be caught eventually.'

'How long do the dots stay on?'

'About a week, but there's more. If you've licked your fingers as you count it there's a reaction with your saliva. It will taste like bitter almonds.'

Rose shrugged. 'So?'

Nic grinned. 'Well, the taste of bitter almonds is also the taste of cyanide. It makes them very paranoid that they think they are being poisoned.'

Rose laughed. 'Dimond told us that she thought Michael may have opened the cash envelope to take a look, and now two thousand dollars are missing. I won't be surprised if he turns up in hospital.'

'That's not nice, Rose. Very funny, but not nice.'

Rose turned to see who had made the comment. It was Dimond.

A week and a half later, Rose and Sandy were sitting on the back deck at West End. Dog was curled on the mat at the top of the stairs, and Goliath was sprawled across the Papasan, all fifteen centimetres of him. Dog suddenly stood up, stretched, and then started cleaning his undercarriage.

'Someone's coming, Rose.'

'Hi, guys. It's us.'

'That's not Dimond's voice. It sounds like Seiko.'

Rose called out. 'Around the back, then up the stairs. Don't mind the cat as he's harmless. He doesn't like Michael, but then nobody does.'

Seiko and Dee-Dee made their way to the deck; both gave Dog a pat on the head and stifled a laugh at the tiny dog in the huge plush chair. They were dressed almost identically, with matching leathers and matching full-face helmets.

Seiko spoke first. 'You've met my sister Dee-Dee; it stands for Data Delivery or Delivery Driver, Deliberately Devious, or whatever Nic wants her to do for him at the time.'

'So, do you both work for him?'

'Sort of. I'm currently doing the night shift for the Police Service, and by day, I help out at the warehouse when I can. It's all part of my alter-ego as a superhero. I've heard you don't have to wear a disguise, just a uniform.'

Sandy nodded. 'You're much too young to be a superhero, seeking truth, justice and the curds and whey.'

Seiko nodded. 'Nic helped me get into the force and helped Dee-Dee into the cyber-crime stuff.'

Dog suddenly stopped licking himself, stood up and shuffled towards the stairs so Seiko moved to the top of the stairs to see who had arrived. It was Nic.

'Hi, guys. It's me, yep, I got bored and came back early.'

Dog bounded down the stairs to greet him, as much as an eight-kilogram cat can bound.

Rose called out again. 'Up here. Seiko and Dee-Dee are here too.'

15

Nic reached the top of the stairs and then sat down in the Papasan, softly rolling Goliath out of the way, allowing Dog, who had followed him back up the stairs, to sit on his lap. 'Great, I need a favour...from all of you.'

Dee-Dee noticed Dog was pawing at Nic's chest for more attention. 'Dog likes you, doesn't he? Must be all the male bonding stuff, the bro-code.'

Nic shrugged. 'As I said, I was bored in Hawaii as there's only so much sun, surf, sea and shopping with your family that a man can put up with.'

Seiko laughed. 'You were going to say something else.'

'No, I wasn't. The Real Estate scam came down quickly. No one got hurt, and everybody's safe, apart from Michael. He called me to find out whether he could die from cyanide ingestion.'

Sandy laughed. 'What did you tell him?'

'I told him it depends on who is trying to poison him.'

Seiko grinned. 'We got lucky as the scam closed quickly once they realised it was over. They confessed and turned on each other. It turned out that Mark Wilson had a gambling problem, but the problem was that he kept winning, and by the time he'd realised he was up instead of down, it was too late. He'd also brought the others into the rental scam.'

The group raised their glasses that another caper had ended so abruptly and Nic continued. 'The next thing we have happening is this Aged Care thing. The initial findings reveal some gaping holes in the budget. Some things can't be explained but mostly it's legal speak gobble-de-gook. Seiko, have you heard anything from the police side?'

'Not really, but I can have a quiet talk with Detective Francis, my appointed mentor. Would it be OK if I set up a meeting with you?'

Nic nodded. 'Sure, but give it a few days to settle the ink on the Real Estate scam stuff. I'd prefer we meet on her turf, so can we make it to Police Headquarters at Roma Street? Have her call the Police Commissioner, Gerry Steldons, in Adelaide as he'll provide her with an insight into Nic Thorn and Associates.' Sandy looked at the group, then at Nic. 'This Aged Care investigation is a heavy one. Are you sure you want Rose and I involved? It's pushing the line between having fun and the law.

'Yep, this is why we have to keep it professional and tight, and it is why I sat on a beach in Hawaii for the last three weeks giving it my special attention.'

They looked at him, and Rose responded. 'Right, apart from the surfing, sun and shopping, what else did you have to do?'

'Well, I had to look after my sisters and parents and ensure they didn't do too much hula dancing in their grassy skirts. My father loves to dance like no one's watching and sing like no one's listening, but sometimes he says things without thinking. He's also a massive Elvis fan. Elvis the Pelvis did three films there, and we even did the famous: 'Elvis Still Lives in Hawaii' Tour three times.'

Dee-Dee looked at him. 'Seiko and I have been there. There's no such Elvis tour.'

'I know, but dear old Dad insisted on calling it that as we drove around to visit the filming sites. There's even a rum and blue curacao drink called the Blue Hawaiian. It was a favourite of Elvis's, so we had to have it at least once, twice, or thrice every time he thought he saw Elvis.'

Sandy smiled. 'I've heard that's a very potent drink, Nic. Are you sure he wasn't just seeing flying pink elephants?'

Nic continued: 'No, but he did make me get up at an open mike night in one of the bars along the Waikiki Beach strip and sing a couple of Elvis songs. It's the first time I've been told to stop singing.'

Rose grinned. 'Oh, poor Nic. Why?' Nic sighed. 'They reckoned my Aussie accent was too strong and ruined them. After all, you know what wise men say...' They waited for him to continue, but he didn't, and finally Sandy responded. 'What's that?'

'Only fools rush in... but they can't help falling in love with.....Hawaii. Anyway, the Aged Care investigation is gaining momentum, and there's even talk of a Royal Commission. We've got to get in there and find out what we can, when we can, about who we can, and if we can get it in the can.'

Rose nodded. 'It all sounds like a can of worms.'

Nic was about to respond when his phone rang, and he managed to manoeuvre Dog and Goliath off this lap and moved downstairs to take the call. They watched him go, and Dee-Dee piped up. 'He does that a lot, doesn't he?'

Rose nodded again. 'I think it's his way that we *don't* hear about all the juicy stuff. It's part of his mantra to protect the family.'

Nic returned and overheard Rose's last comment. 'Thanks Rosa Giardino. It's just got a little easier for us now as that call was from the Head of the Audit Team, and we have been approved to bring in another employee. So, Dee-Dee, you'll now be known as Dee-Dee. I'm working on my surname....I think I'll use Holmes, as in Sherlock.'

'That's too cliché, Nic. I want something better, less Detective, more superhero.'

'Ok, then, Dee-Dee Prince.'

Rose interrupted the banter. 'That's Wonder Woman's surname, Diane Prince.' The group all looked at her; even Dog raised his head. 'Yes, that's another TV series re-run I've watched. Lynda Carter was great. Sandy has a Lasso of Truth around here somewhere. She tried it once, but it didn't quite work.'

Nic grinned. 'They've just done a re-make with Gal Godot, Rose.'

'Really? I must have missed that.'

Nic looked at her. 'And you call yourself a super-hero? There were so many super people in those new films that they started making them up like Soupa-man, Minestrone-girl, and my favourite, Vegan Vegie the Vulcan.'

'I don't think so, Nic, you're making it up yourself.'

'Well, Seiko is a policewoman; and they're allowed to lie a little to get their man, or woman as the case may be.' Nic then stood up, much to Dog's annoyance. 'I've got somewhere else to be so I'll get Chewy to update you with the details about the Aged Care stuff and be in touch. Oh, by the way, have any of you been to Sydney lately?' Seiko and Dee-Dee smiled while Rose and Sandy shook their heads.

'OK, good to know. I'll talk about that later. Elvis has now left the building.' Nic moved down the stairs and, a couple of minutes later, they heard the growl of a Mustang startup. The group stood up and moved towards the balcony, trying to glimpse the car.

Rose leaned forward. 'I didn't hear that car before?' Meantime, the car engine was still throbbing. Sandy added. 'Me either.'

They stepped down the stairs and moved around to gain a better look. Nic was sitting in a Toyota Prius, holding his phone out the window. He waved and motioned to put his foot on the accelerator, and the throb of a Mustang sounded out again. He laughed at them, gave a wave, and drove off.

Rose yelled out over the din. 'You dope, we'll get a noise complaint from the neighbours that Dog has been purring too loudly.'

They moved back to the deck and sat down again, then Rose looked at Dee-Dee and Seiko. 'So how long have you guys been working with Nic?'

Dee-Dee took a breath. 'About four years. I've heard so much about you and Sandy so I thought we should meet. I've been watching your expenses, you don't spend much do you?'

Sandy responded. 'Well, it's all a bit odd. He gives us the cards to spend money on, but it still feels weird. He doesn't pay us any wages, though.'

Dee-Dee looked at them. 'Yes, he does. There's a monthly transfer going into your bank accounts.'

Sandy shook her head. 'What bank accounts? We've never given any bank account details to him.'

'But you've provided him with a copy of your passports and driver's licences, and that's all you need to open an online account, even in someone else's name.'

Rose nodded. 'We would be earning interest on the accounts, and they'd show up when we did our tax returns. The Tax File Number stuff would link it all together.'

'Have you been doing Annual Tax returns, Rose?'

'No, well yes. I get a distribution from my family trust, but the family's Accountant does the return.'

'What about you, Sandy?'

'I don't earn anything apart from a tiny bit of bank interest on my accounts with the banks, and my Dad does look after all that.'

Dee-Dee nodded. 'So Nic could have been depositing money into your bank accounts for the last year or so.'

Sandy shrugged. 'Has he been doing that?' Dee-Dee nodded again. 'But don't worry; he did that to me too for the first three years I worked here. I kept asking him who this 'Deidre Doolittle' was and when I would meet her. He finally gave up and handed me an employee pass with my picture.

Dee-Dee took a breath. 'Well, that was the first and only time I decided to quit. It was sneaky, and I wouldn't say I liked it. But then he gave me a student pass for the University of Queensland to study Cyber Crime. I'd won a scholarship and had a sponsor too, Nic, so I punched him in the shoulder instead.'

Seiko nodded at her sister. 'And he helped me get into the Police Academy. I was a bit lost after leaving University. I'd been studying Psychology and Criminology. I intended to take a gap year, but I met Nic in a bar one night, and we started talking about serving in the Armed Forces. It was odd. I thought he was good-looking, but he was more like an interested big brother. We talked, drank some fine scotch, and he told me about some contacts he had at the Wacol Police Barracks. Two days later, I got a call.'

Rose smiled. 'Nic is an enigma, isn't he?'

Seiko nodded. 'Yes, and one thing that has stayed with me all these years. He even came to my Police Graduation, and I introduced him to.....Wow, I was about to say Dee-Dee's real name.'

Seiko and Dee-Dee got up and went to leave, but Sandy stopped them. 'Hey, I just realised something. Nic mentioned Sydney, but there is more than just the one in New South Wales. I think there's one in Canada and the United States. Woo-hoo. Let's get our passports ready.'

The two sisters laughed, moved down the stairs and then Dee-Dee turned back. 'There's one in Vanuatu too. I went hiking on a volcano when I was there.'

Rose and Sandy didn't have to wait long to know the others were on the move as the growling throb of two Harley Davidson's going up the street was undeniable. 'Harley Twins, by the sounds of them.'

Sandy shook her head. 'There are three years between the sisters.'

'I was talking about the motorbikes; they are both Harley-Davidsons.'

Sandy grinned. 'I guess I knew that. I was going with a guy who thought about buying one but he settled on a Yamaha Virago instead. He rode up on it and tried to convince me they were just as good. I looked at it, shut the front door, and returned inside laughing. I never saw him again after that.'

Rose nodded. 'Don't you just hate it when you are taken for a ride that turns out to be nothing more than a cute and fluffy rodent doing circles in a plastic wheel? Anyway, what do you think of Dee-Dee and Seiko? They're only a couple of years younger than us, yet we've spent the last couple of years travelling around Australia with Nic, and they haven't.'

'Maybe we should ask Nic about it?'

'Maybe we should ask them?'

'Maybe we should ask ourselves?'

'Maybe we should just ignore it altogether?'

'Agreed.'

Rose smiled. 'Did you really look at the Aged Care Reports that Chewy sent?'

Sandy grinned. 'No. I got access to the printed reports and Nic was right; they are heavy reading. I went through it all and made some notes, and there are some blatant discrepancies. A couple of companies seem to be getting paid much quicker than the rest. It's all in the Creditor Ledgers. Government departments normally pay around ninety days after invoicing, but one group seems to be getting paid within forty-five days. Chewy did on-line company searches on the and they all seem to have the same complex structure. He's still trying to find out who the actual owners are. Follow the money; isn't that the key?'

'That sounds like a lot of work. How will we make sure this investigation keeps the fun level up like the others we've done so far?'

'No idea, but how was the look on Nic's face when we herded the reindeer into the kitchen, and it turned out to be the Queensland Aged Care Minister and his side-kick?'

'That was classic stuff up, yet Nic takes whatever we do or don't do in his stride. I think it's quite endearing of him, but there has to be more to all of this.'

'You worry too much, Rose.'

'I know, but at least I've got my happy face on now.'

'It looks the same as your normal face.'

'Hey, I'm trying, you know.' Rose was about to make another face to test the point when her phone rang. She saw the name; it was a call from her new Aged Care Audit Team supervisor. 'Rosa Giardino speaking, how can I help you?'

'Hello Rosa, it's Carmel De Soto calling from the Queensland Heath Audit Team. I'm just making sure that you are ready to join our team next Monday. Did you receive my message that we've relocated from Brisbane to Sydney, and the office is on Macquarie Street, on the corner of Phillip Lane? It didn't seem a good idea to audit a Queensland Government Health Department if the Auditors are based in Brisbane. Where are you living now?'

Rose put her hand over the phone speaker. 'Quick, Sandy, name a suburb of Sydney.'

'I don't know; I haven't been there for a while....um...Paddington....I think there's one in Sydney.' Sandy started to google the suburb on the phone but could only bring up Paddington in Brisbane.

'Oh, sorry, Carmel. I missed that; you were asking where I live is Syndey?'

'Yes.'

'I'm in Paddington, near the football stadium.'

'Ok, wow, great spot, but very expensive though. Anyway, we'll see you next Monday.'

Rose hung up. 'Sandy, is there a football stadium in Paddington?'

'Yes, that was lucky. It's the Sydney Cricket Ground; the Sydney Swans play there. It's their home ground.'

'Good to know, thanks. What are the Sydney Swans?'

'Aussie Rules, rule Rose, but I don't think you have to worry, as Nic hasn't told us where we'll be based in Sydney. You could just say you relocated.'

16

They rang Nic, and Rose put the phone on speaker. 'Hey, it's us. I just had Carmel De Soto on the phone. By the way, when I had the interview for the job what did I tell her I was bringing to her team?'

'Sorry, Rose....I'll send your C.V. to you to have a read. She was very impressed and I put in a good word when she rang me for a reference.'

'When did she do that?'

'About a month ago, just before I discovered they were relocating the Audit Team from Brisbane to Sydney. The interview was all done via Zoom. I had my sister stand in for you at short notice; I hope you didn't mind.'

'Was that Nicole, the one that lives in Sydney? That won't work, What if they recognise her at the cosmetic stand at David Jones in Sydney's Pitt Street Mall?'

'No, it was the other one that lives in Murrayville, Victoria. My twin. She's worked with me before on some of the early investigations and was happy to help out a damsel in distress.'

Rose shook her head. 'I wasn't distressed, I didn't even know about it.'

'No, you didn't, but she was in Brisbane and it only took a couple of moments to set up with Chewy's help.'

'Let me guess, your sister has auburn hair cut into a bob, wears thick-framed black glasses, and looks like Velma from Scooby Doo.'

'Wow, Rose, I thought you'd never met her?'

'Well, at least I know what she looks like now. Me, dressed up as Velma.'

'Not quite Rose, she was wearing a disguise. She was you, dressed as you.'

'Damn you, Nic.'

'Anyhow, where am I based in Sydney? I told her Paddington.'

'Good guess, but it's Darlinghurst. We're using a property with three different street addresses, but we're all under the same roof. Dee-Dee and you will be sharing a two-bedroom apartment, and Sandy and I have a one-bedroom sitter each.'

'So, the premise is that Dee-Dee and I have worked together before, and you and Sandy have been brought in as external consultants?'

'Yes, as I said, pretty simple.'

'Maybe for you.'

Nic responded. 'It's worked so far. I've brought you two into the last eight investigations, and none of those have got too complicated.'

Rose added. 'Yes, and thanks for that, but this time we are pretending to be people, on the pretence of knowing what we are supposed to know, without giving up things in the investigation that others are not supposed to know, that we know.'

Nic took a breath. 'Now you've gone and done it, Rose. You've made it complicated. Dee-Dee will be there with you. Just nod, drink lots of coffee and say, "Do you concur?" if anyone asks you a question.'

Rose shook her head nervously; then Sandy motioned that she had a question, and leaned toward the phone. 'I heard something about me and you sharing an apartment.'

'Not quite, and by the way, your name for this caper is Sandy Shaw. It's spelt differently from the English singer from the 60s, but the sound is the same and close enough to confuse anyone searching Linked In. When you Google the name, all that comes up is the actress.'

'Good to know. Anything else?'

'Yes, you guys have the choice of flying down with me next week or riding down with Dee-Dee.'

'Riding down?'

'Yep, on the back of her Harley.'

'Our luggage won't fit.'

'She can get a sidecar for the luggage.'

'We will both fly with you, thank you very much.'

Nic continued. 'OK. I'll send you some more stuff to read before we leave. The flight leaves at four, and when we land, we'll head straight to the apartments. Dee-Dee will be going down earlier to set things up.'

Rose nodded. 'OK, Sandy has already gone through the myriad of Queensland Health reports. Do you want me to make my own notes?'

'Yep, you might need to appear to have your head around the numbers'

They leaned forward. 'Anything else, Charlie?'

'Yes, my Angels. I heard you've sold the Morgan. Are you looking for another car to flip?'

Rose shrugged. 'Maybe. I'm thinking of finding a Rolls Royce Silver Shadow for under twenty thousand, then getting a paisley paint job done. It's coming up to John Lennon's birthday, and there could be an opportunity if I pitch it correctly. There could be a demand for one from a The Beatles Fan club member. I've even started listening to their music too. They sing many songs about love, don't they? Go on, ask me a Beatles trivia question.'

'OK, where did they play their last outdoor concert?'

'That's an easy one. When they stopped playing live, although I've seen a vision of them playing on the roof of a building, was it that one?

'Something like that. It was Candlestick Park, California, 29th August 1966.'

'Cripes, I don't even think you were born then, Nic.'

'Yep, I was born on the 9th of October 1980. Damn, I almost fell for that one.'

Sandy called out. 'Yes, Nic, now we know when to order your birthday cake and buy the socks and hankies.'

Rose piped up. 'Hey, that's John Lennon's birth-date, just forty years before, in 1940. Is that really yours? Hang on, that makes you nearly forty, and yet you don't look a day over mid-thirties.'

'Umm...I know I'm so complicated, and yet, still, I look so young and youthful. It must be all the manly moisturisers I use.'

'Say goodbye, Nic. We have to start planning for your birthday. Would you like your party at the Alma Park Zoo? You could get your face painted and have a pony ride. We'll see you at the airport around three. Let us know if you need anything else.'

'Thanks, guys, I think.'

They disconnected the call and Sandy grinned. 'Wow, so you know what that means?'

'Yes, I'm rooming with someone I don't know who may or may not hold a grudge against us for stealing Nic away, whom I need to work with in something I know nothing about.'

Sandy shook her head and googled "October Star Signs." 'Nope. It means Nic is a Libra, and that explains a lot. Listen to this: Librans are peaceful, impartial, and constantly require company. That sounds like Nic.'

Rose nodded, then googled "October Star Sign" herself but used a different browser site. 'OK, this one says Librans are wise and like to impress people they talk to.' Rose then Googled her Star sign, and read it out. It said similar things as October.

Sandy leaned back. 'I didn't think you're a Libran, your birthday is in December, so that makes you a Capricorn.'

'I know, but I'm on the cusp which makes me dangerous.'

Rose started singing. "Torn between two-star signs, feeling like a fool, you know what it's like when you can't stop a drool."

Sandy shook her head. 'That's not the song lyrics.'

Rose sighed. 'I can't remember everything, you know. I'm nearly thirty, and it all goes downhill from there.'

'That's not fair. I'm already thirty, and I haven't started going downhill, not yet, anyway. Mind you,

I've left the apex in the rear mirror already. Imagine if we were as old as Nic?'

'I know. I think we should have another drink to that.'

'What's that?'

'Not being as old as Nic.'

It was now Friday afternoon. Rose and Sandy were waiting for Nic at the Brisbane Domestic Airport. He was late, and it was very unlike him, and when he arrived he was looking a little stressed. Again, very unlike him.

Rose looked at him. 'So what's up, Nic? This isn't like you...you're always prim and proper, smartly dressed, and desirable. Well, that's what I've heard anyway.'

Nic shrugged. 'You're right, and I'm a little off my game. It's getting really serious this stuff. My game is usually a couple of windbags kicking around a ball full of wind, and I'm the umpire in control. This one looks like the major league, and I've lost my whistle. Chewy has delved a little more into the ownership of the companies that are getting favourable treatment for invoice overpayments. He's tracked them through the company shareholders, then onto Unit Trusts, but still not down to the individuals, so we're not quite there yet.'

Rose looked at him. 'This is all super squirrelly spy stuff. Would you like us to step back on this one?'

Nic shook his head. 'Not sure yet, but we can only take it as far as we can, and if we have to step back, we call in the big guns, but I don't know who they are or where I would find them.'

Sandy shook her head. 'So, do we keep going?'

Nic tapped his nose. 'But it may not be a secret as you think. The deeper we go, the murkier it seems to get, but the light is beginning to shine on those hiding in their rabbit holes. So let's get on the plane, get to Sydney, and then we'll go through it all with Dee-Dee.'

17

An hour and a half later, they disembarked, collected their luggage and Dee-Dee was waiting for them in the foyer. 'Welcome to Sydney.' They went outside, climbed into a maxi-taxi, and headed for Darlinghurst. The apartment complex was situated on a small land allotment. Access was via three separate doors, the door to the two-room unit that faced the main road, whilst the others had their access on the road, either side. Three apartments, three separate street addresses, and three off-street garage spaces. They went into the apartment that Dee-Dee and Rose were to share first.

Sandy took a look around. 'Wow, this place is amazing....with a capital 'zing', Nic. Is it yours?'

'Sort of.'

'Another one of your property projects, then?'

Nic smiled. 'Sort of....they are Dee-Dee and Seiko's apartments. So, whilst you guys are working with me on the inside of the investigation, you can be working with me on the inside with fixing the apartments. Win, win, I'd say.'

'For you, Nic, but for us, it's like too much work, whatever way you look at it.'

Nic continued: 'Seiko will be down here soon too. It will be like the last Spice Girls reunion tour, which Posh said she was too busy to sign up for.'

They moved through the apartment, and it certainly needed a little work, but the kitchen was semi-completed. Rose went through the space, opened the bedroom doors, and came back shaking her head. 'There's only one bathroom in here. I can't stay in a place where I have to share a bathroom.'

The trio looked at Nic, but Sandy spoke first. 'So what will you be doing whilst we're toiling over a hammer, chisel, and a bucket of smashed tiles?'

Nic smiled. 'Supervising as usual. It's what I'm renowned for. Anyway, we can look at all of this later. I think we need to get together and discuss the Audit.'

Rose nodded. 'Good idea. Seeing I've no idea what they expect of me or what I can offer.'

'Yep, there is that. A typical audit comprises four stages: planning, fieldwork, reporting, and follow-up. In this case, we'll be doing the fieldwork, so we have to keep it under some sort of image that we know what we're doing. Sandy and I will arrive later for a formal meet and greet. Then we'll do lunch.'

Rose sighed. 'What do I do after lunch?'

Nic rubbed his chin. 'We could always come up with an emergency and have to leave.' Rose nodded. 'When did you last speak to Carmel De Soto?'

'I have a conference call on Friday with her, then we are due to fly down early Monday morning for the meet and greet at one of the restaurants on the promenade by the Sydney Opera House for lunch.'

'But you're both already here.'

'I know, and you think you're confused.' Nic's phone rang as he was about to continue: 'This is Nicolas Thyme speaking. Yes, thank you for calling Carmel. How can I help you?'

He paused for a response. 'OK, we'll be down on Monday and meet up at the restaurant as discussed.' Nic put the phone onto the loudspeaker, placed it face up on the kitchen bench, and held his finger to his lips to indicate to the others to be quiet.

Carmel continued. 'We've encountered a problem with the office space and the Wi-Fi is not yet fully available so won't be able to set up on Monday. The tech guys are at least a week away before finalising it.'

Nic responded. 'OK, I can handle that. Sandra and I can work from our hotel apartments. Will that suit you?'

'Sure, and thank you.' Carmel hesitated, then continued. 'Oh, there is another issue. The office we've been offered is 'hot-desking', which means first come, first served. Anyone who doesn't get a desk has to work from home. So, with Dee-Dee and Rosa arriving simultaneously, we've only got one desk available.'

'That's fine, Carmel. Please call Rosa and see if she can work from our apartment too. Dee-Dee will come alone. Anything else, Carmel?'

'No, that's it. I'll see you on Monday for lunch.'

'Yes, I can cover that. My team of four, and your team of four.'

'Well, about that too, budget cuts and everything. My team of four is now a team of two, but you'll save on lunch.'

'OK, see you then.' Nic disconnected and looked at his group. 'Now that's an interesting change of plans. Is everyone good with all that?'

Sandy nodded. 'Actually, I've got a serious question, Nic. Why are you using the name Nicolas Thyme again? You used it in Adelaide with the invoice scamming caper.'

'Yep, I'm having to cut costs. Chewy sent me a budget forecast for our Work in Progress and my expenses don't seem to be adding up. I think I'll call in an auditor.' Rose shook her head. 'Seriously, Nic?'

'Nup, it's just that Chewy said it was easier to change the details on my Nicolas Thyme profile rather than set up another one. I'm running out of names.'

Rose added. 'Sure, but I can think of a few more like Nick Toff and Nick Neighm'

'Thanks for the offer, Rose *Bush*.'

Dee-Dee looked at Rose 'Hey, I just realised you married Michael Bush.'

Rose grimaced. 'Well, it was the fault of George W. and George H., that's the POTUS Dad and son duo. Michael had spread the rumour around the school that his Bush family was directly related to them. Then it got into my Father's head that his way of increasing trading opportunities with the United States of America was to make me available.' Rose shivered at the recollections.

Dee-Dee chuckled. 'I love some of the quotes from George W. *'They misunderestimated me'* and the classic one, *'I know how hard it is for you to put food on your family.'* I used to have them spinning around on my screen saver while studying at Uni.'

Rose gathered her composure. 'Yep, good old Michael 'Bush Turkey' Bush. He used it for a long time. I did a genealogy search and discovered he was only related to George Bush from Mother England., and he had arrived in Australia as a convict after being caught for stealing a box of rocks.'

Dee-Dee nodded. 'Was that before or after you were told to marry him, Rose?'

'It was six months before, but Father chose to ignore me anyway. The deal went south, the marriage went north, Michael went west, and I headed east.'

Dee-Dee piped up. 'East?'

Sandy interjected. 'Yes, three days later, I joined Rose in Auckland, and we had a lovely holiday in New Zealand at Michael's expense.'

18

Nic left early in the morning to do some reconnaissance on the audit office and make the lunch reservation at the restaurant for Monday. He left a note saying he was expecting to be away all day.

It was now around 5 pm, and the others had spent the afternoon smashing through the adjoining wall and framing up the door, at least that's what they told Nic they had been doing, but the truth was they saw a builder working down the road and coaxed him to do the work. The builder was tidying up the rubble and looked over to Rose.

'I've got about half an hour before I'm finished painting the door. When did you say the ugly landlord would be back? Surely he didn't expect you three to do all this work and not pay you anything?'

Rose nodded. 'I know, right?'

'Rose, be nice.'

Rose swung around, and Nic was standing there. 'Hiya Doug, it's been a while. Are you still doing the building pre-inspections? The trio looked at him and the builder nodded.

'Nope. I closed the business down when I retired but then got bored at home. The missus had me going to the movies, museums, and libraries. I told her I don't like to sit still that long, and I don't like reading. What else could I do?'

Sandy piped up. 'You could have tried buying a caravan and doing the grey nomad stuff.'

'Hey, that's not nice; I don't have any grey hair.'

Doug took off his cap and waved it at them. 'I may be bald, but I don't have any grey hair. Besides, do I look like I could spend my time living out of a metal box on wheels? I've built and fixed up brick boxes all my life, and they don't make those vans big enough yet. I would need at least a four-bedroom one. One room for me, one for the missus, one for the dog and to store all my work tools, and one for ... well, just a spare.'

Nic handed him a copy of the renovation plans and Doug gave them the once over. 'I'll get my crew to come in tomorrow, and we'll have it finished early next week sometime. Does that suit you?'

'Thanks, mate.'

'Oh, by the way, do you still get called 'The Batman?''

'Not really, but these two reckon I could be, and maybe I am?' Nic looked over to Rose and Sandy

'Have you ever seen Batman and me in the same room together? They both shrugged.

Doug stood up, stepped out of his overalls, and folded them neatly into a knapsack. He had jeans and a tight-fitting t-shirt underneath and showed off his solid torso. He saluted and left. 'See you in the morning.'

Dee-Dee turned to Nic. 'So, where should we go if they are renovating?'

'Good point, Dee-Dee; I don't think we could all squeeze into the single-bedroom unit even though it's almost finished. I guess I'll have to find somewhere else for us. Any ideas?'

'Not really. We don't live in Sydney, but I can ask around. I've heard the Sandy and Rose only like five-star, and I've seen the Hotel tariffs around here.'

Nic nodded. 'Leave it to me, I'll make a call.' He walked over to the fridge and grabbed a beer from it. 'Drinks, anyone?'

They all declined.

'Nope, thanks, Nic, we've got work to do.'

'What work?'

'Reading through the Audit reports for Monday's induction.'

'Haven't you guys been doing that all day?'

Rose shook her head. 'Oh, no, once the repairs started, we'd decided to take a walk and discover

Sydney town. Then took a ride on the Manly ferry and did girly stuff, like having our nails done.'

They held out their hands for Nic to inspect. 'Nice.'

Sandy added. 'And we didn't spend too much of your money either.' Nic ignored the comment. 'So, how much of the renovations did you do before they started?'

They all looked sheepish, and Rose responded. 'Well, you left around seven, Doug came in at eight, and there was simply no time to do anything.'

'Did you talk a budget with him then, Dee-Dee?'

Dee-Dee nodded. 'He said if we pay cash, he'll keep it under twenty-five thousand dollars as long as we buy the taps and stuff. We're using the same tiles in the kitchen as the bathrooms. The cedar-wood floors will be re-sanded for about fifteen hundred dollars per unit. Any more questions?'

'Nup, I'll just go and make a call. I've got a good idea of where we can stay, and it has very close views of the water. I hope none of you gets sea-sick.'

Rose looked at him. 'I'm not sleeping in a sea-plane.'

Nic moved outside to make the call and Dee-Dee looked over to Rose and Sandy 'Are you getting nervous about Monday, Rose?'

'Not really, but I wouldn't be surprised if Nic sets up a soiree at the Opera House, and I didn't bring a little black dress.'

Sandy nodded. 'Me neither, so we might just have to go shopping again.'

Nic ambled back in after about 15 minutes. 'OK, it's all set up. We've got four units. Dee-Dee and Seiko will share one. Food and drinks are complimentary, there's a swimming pool, a gym and daily room service are on board....'

They looked at him. 'Onboard?'

'Yep, we're staying on board one of the Cruise Ships currently moored at the Sydney Cove Overseas Passenger Terminal.'

Rose looked at him. 'You're not serious?'

'Yep. I had lunch with the Cruise Director, and he said if I'd ever like some cheap accommodation on board, to let him know. There is a catch though as they're running a training school during our stay, so it might not be up to their normal standard. So gather your stuff, and we can head down there now if you like. They'll even arrange a courtesy bus to collect us.'

Dee-Dee nodded. 'I told Seiko to stay in Brisbane, I thought it might be better if she remained up there with her eyes and ears on the ground. We need someone up there to check things out. She won't be undercover, just a concerned citizen looking around.' Nic smiled. 'Why I didn't think of that. I must be getting too old for all this stuff.'

They re-packed their luggage, Nic arranged the courtesy bus and about forty minutes later, they were being directed along the gangplank into the belly of the beast, known as 'The Prince of The Sea.' After giving Nic a secret handshake, the Cruise Director welcomed them aboard.

The three women looked at the performance, and Nic nodded over to them. 'This is Rose, Sandy and Dee-Dee. They are working with me on the Queensland Health Audit investigation.'

They looked at him, wondering why he'd told the man about that part, but Nic soon alleviated their concern: 'I've known this big guy since my Afghanistan days. Let me introduce you to Julian McCoy. We called him "Big Julie" after the Cruise Director on the Love Boat TV show from the '80s. It was one of the only re-runs of the shows we could pick up along on the TV station whilst serving over there.'

The big man moved over to them. He stood about two metres tall and shook their hands. His hands were as big as baseball gloves, and he shrugged his massive shoulders. 'What else could I do, I was destined to be a Cruise Director once I left the war in my wake.'

Nic grinned. 'Touché, Big Julie. So, where are our cabins, mid-ship, aft, starboard or whatever the other shippy names are for these little rooms you call living quarters in these floating behemoths?'

'Hey, that's not fair; we've got you in the best suites at the aft. I have a three-bedroom cabin for each of you. There's nothing to look at apart from the Sydney Harbour Bridge on one side and the Opera House on the other. You might just be impressed.'

The baggage handlers had already collected their luggage, so they headed further inside. Big Julie showed them where the nearest bar was, then the second bar, and went outside to the pool area bar. Then, they went back inside to the casino bar and through to the stage area, where they had the live shows, and there was another bar.

On the way back, the group passed a hairdressing salon for women only. The door showed a "Complimentary Styling Bar.' Big Julie turned around and looked at his little troupe. 'We don't the men in as they get confused and come to ask for a drink.' Finally, he led them towards their suites.

Nic was on the port side, whilst the other suites were along the starboard. Their luggage had been delivered, and it was all unpacked and stored away. Nic peered into the salon window as they returned to one of the interior lounge areas. It was currently empty. 'Hey Rose, I hope you realise the Hairdressing Salon will soon be open for business. We still have to get your hair cut into a bob and dyed auburn for the 'Velma' look for the office on Monday. You have to look something like your ID pass, at least.'

'Damn you, Nic, I thought you'd forgotten.'

Nic brought up the ID pass on his phone and showed it to Big Julie. 'Yep, that can be done. I'll even do it myself if you like.'

Rose looked at him. 'Are you a hairstylist as well as a Cruise Director?'

He shook his head. 'Nope, but we're going through the rehearsals on the ship at the moment. I'm the lead role in 'Sweeney Todd, The Demon Barber of Fleet Street. Snip, snip.'

They all laughed, except for Rose. 'Dinner is being served in the main dining hall. Would you like to freshen up or come with me now?' Nic responded. 'Let's make it in an hour. I've got to return a phone call from Detective Audrey Francis; she's Seiko's police liaison in Brisbane. It looks like she's been assigned to the case, so it will be interesting to see how this investigation goes.'

Big Julie looked around. 'Righto, then. A quick lesson on getting around the ship, it's pretty easy. You go up or down, port or starboard, fore or aft, and when you find you're at the sides of the ship, don't step off. It's a long way down, and you might get wet.' He then saluted at Nic and walked away.

At around 8 p.m., they were assembled in the dining room with sixty other guests queued in the area, waiting to be seated. Nic's group was eventually shown to the Captain's Table, much to the other guests' annoyance. They sat, and meal orders were taken. Alcohol was complimentary, so Rose ordered two glasses of Chardonnay. Nic and Dee-Dee decided on scotch whiskey.

An elderly statesman approached them, stood at the table, and they assumed he was the Captain. 'Good evening, ladies and gentlemen. I am British Naval Officer, Captain Edward Smith, and I welcome you aboard. It's my titanic struggle to make sure you all have a good time tonight.'

Rose looked at him. 'Wow, so you survived the 1912 disaster. By my reckoning, you would be over a hundred and fifty years old.'

The man smiled. 'Why, thank you, young lady, I know whom to have as our Trivia Queen tomorrow. I've tried it on two other tables tonight, and no one got the connection.'

The man remained standing. 'So, you are friends with Big Julie, our Cruise Director. I do hope that you like your seven-night stay on board. You are free to move around, but as we are technically at sea, please remember you are not allowed to disembark.' The Captain moved away to talk to the other guests. 'I'll be back, but don't worry about holding my seat as no one wants my job anyway.' He laughed at his joke.

Nic nodded, then whispered, 'Oops, sorry guys, I forgot to tell you about that part.' Dee-Dee looked at him. 'So how are we supposed to turn up for work on Monday? Swim?'

Meantime, Big Julie came over and sat down in the Captain's chair. 'I've got some good news and some bad news. Good news: I've managed to get you disembarking early Monday morning to do that Aged Care thing. The bad news is it's the early shift, at four o'clock in the morning, but at least you can get off with the fifty or so bags of dirty laundry.'

19

It was still dark and very early, when Nic went along the cabin doors, ensuring the others were awake. Rose and Dee-Dee emerged fully dressed. However, Sandy was not answering the door, so he rang her room. She eventually opened the door but was still dressed in pyjamas. 'Hey, I don't need to start today until after lunch. Why are you expecting me to get up so early?'

'Well, you're right, but I was hoping you would come back with us to the apartments and supervise the builders whilst we're doing our thing at the Aged Care thing.'

'Wow, I've already had a promotion. I've only been working with you for eighteen months, and finally, a pay rise to supervisor.'

'Who said anything about that?'

'Well, you know that those who can't do teach. Besides, I was thinking of ordering room service for breakfast.'

'Normally, yes, but I don't even think the kitchen is open at four in the morning.'

Sandy grumbled a bit more, shut the door and emerged a couple of minutes later dressed top to tail in a 'onesie'. It was a dark purple woollen hooded Jumpsuit with a balaclava that she folded down over her head.

Nic looked her over. 'Did you just put your pyjamas back on?'

'No, I only wear Chanel No. 5 to bed. This is to sneak off the ship. I assume we have to climb into a rubber ducky and get offshore that way in the darkness.'

Nic laughed. 'Nup, we are going off as laundry people, over the gangplank like normal people trying to sneak off a ship, dressed as laundry people.'

Sandy nodded. 'Hang on then; I have to take these off.'

Nic looked down at her feet. Sandy was wearing flippers, peeled them off and threw them back into her room.

The group headed off to the laundry area, met Big Julie along the way, and were each shown a trolley full of laundry to wheel offboard from the lower deck. Nic nodded. 'Thanks, mate. Are you coming off as well?'

'Nope, they might notice the Cruise Director has gone AWOL. You four should be OK, maybe not

Sandy dressed as The Phantom, she might need to change into something less something.'

Sandy nodded. 'I'll be OK, but thanks for checking. I am the ghost who walks so that no one will notice me. Has anyone seen Devil and Hero?'

'Who are they, Sandy?'

'There are my wolf and my little horsey, but the other thing is The Phantom doesn't have superpowers. I've just got strength, charm, and wit. Much like Nic.'

Nic smiled. 'I have superpowers. Like being able to leap to conclusions in a single bound, jump high when I see a spider and run faster than a liquorice bullet.'

Rose then lugged a laundry bag over her shoulder and pushed one of the laundry trolleys along the gangplank. 'Come on Spidey-geek, and Purple Syrple Girl, we've got to get this stuff moving. You too, Dee-Dee-Do-right.'

They entered the ship terminal and deposited the laundry into a waiting truck. A couple of the drivers gave the group the once over but said nothing apart from one comment about it being too early to see a walking purple carrot.

Nic hailed a taxi, and they returned to the apartments. 'We've got about two hours before the builders arrive, so you can all go back to bed for a while or an early morning run.'

Rose looked at him. 'The beds have been re-moved, and there's nowhere to sleep apart from the bath. Besides that, we didn't bring our pj's.'

'Well, you can take turns sleeping in the bath. John Lennon did it in that Norwegian Wood song, which didn't affect him. Any other ideas? It's a beautiful early Saturday morning in Sydney; the sun's just rising, the birds are waking, and the late-night revellers are chowing down on their second souvlaki.'

'That's disgusting, Nic.'

'Which part Dee-Dee?'

'Everyone knows it's a greasy hamburger that's the best hangover cure, not some freshly prepared lamb and falafel roll.'

'Speaking from experience?'

Nic shook his head. 'Oh, no. We passed a Burger joint on the way, and that's what's written on their front window. It was a big window.'

'All right then, we're already awake and all at your disposal. Have you got any ideas?'

'We could go to the zoo or Manly or take a ferry ride up to Parramatta. On second thought, Sandy and I aren't supposed to have arrived until Monday morning, so we should get out of the CBD.'

Nic stepped out of earshot and made a call, then told the group to wait until the builder arrived so they could go over the job. They didn't have to wait long as Doug arrived, so they stepped outside, and a dark blue Toyota MPV was waiting for them.

Nic opened the door, and the driver nodded to the group. It had seven seats, and the windows were darkened with black film. Nic nodded to the driver, then sat in the front passenger seat, and the others stepped in through the sliding door.

'This is Syd, guys. He'll be our driver for the next two days.'

Rose looked at him. 'Let me guess. His name is Sydney, as in our Sydney driver?'

'Yo, ma'am. Syd's the name, and driving in Sydney is my game. My game is darts, but you get the point. I've been doing both for forty years or so.' He tapped the brim of his chauffeur cap. 'So, where are we off to today, Mr Thyme?'

'The Featherdale Wildlife Park, thanks, Syd.'

'Got it, Boss. It's about a forty-minute drive, depending on the traffic. Is there anything I need to know about our passengers? Like, are they back-seat drivers? Or ex-Grand Prix drivers? Or worse, that they are better drivers than me? I tend to crash fairly early and all this driving makes me sleepy.'

Sandy piped up from the back seat. 'How many crashes have you had, Syd?'

He pulled into the traffic. 'Well, young lady, it depends on what you classify as a crash. Is a bingle a crash? A smash, a crash? Was it my fault? Was it their fault? Was it no one's fault? As long as no one gets hurt, apart from pride, was it a crash in the first place?'

Nic nodded. 'Yep, like they say, if a tree falls in a forest and no one hears it scream, did it find the bear?'

'Exactly, mate. I saw a bear once; it didn't have any ears. Does that make it a 'b'?'

Rose shouted from the back seat: 'Stop it, you two.'

Nic nodded. 'Sorry, Rose, it's just that I'm eager to cuddle a koala or kiss a kangaroo, and it's my birthday.'

'Nic, you told us you were born on October nine. We've even ordered the cake.'

'Sorry about that, guys, but today is my birthday.'

Rose called out. 'What's the date then, Nic?'

'Um, the 5th or the 6^{th,} maybe. I don't know. I'm just another year older, and it's scaring me.'

Rose added. 'So, it's not today then either, is it?'

'Nup, but we can pretend, can't we?' He broke into song. '*We're going to the zoo, zoo, zoo. How about you, you, you?*'

'Please stop, Nic.'

'Singing or driving, Rose?'

'Both. We're almost there, and you'll scare the animals. Both the ones that live in and outside the zoo walls.'

The group kept silent for a while, and they had been motoring for about thirty minutes, taking a leisurely route through the suburbs. Syd looked over to Nic, then nodded towards the rear-view mirror.

'Call me paranoid, Nic, but can we have a tail?'

'Could be, but pretty unusual, unless we've picked up a kangaroo. What's up?'

'Well, the white Toyota Camry behind us. It has been about six cars behind for a while, and I've been going pretty slowly, sitting well under the speed limit. We're in Sydney, and everyone's in a hurry to get wherever. Anyway, that car has to be going slower than me.'

Rose overheard. 'So why is that suspicious? Who else have you been driving around to make you jump to that conclusion?'

'Well, I don't just drive for Nic. Let me see; there was that red-headed guy from England most recently.'

'Wow, Prince Harry or Ed Sheeran?'

'Nope. I think he said his name was Sir Ronald McDonald, from Scotland. Sorry, I'm sworn to the Secret Chauffer Code of Chastity and can't mention any names.' Nic chortled. 'So, back the tail, Syd, have you managed to get the licence plates yet?'

'Nope, not yet, sorry. They've kept far enough away.'

'OK, move out to the right lane, then take the next exit to the left. If there's no space, do it further up the road instead.'

'Roger that.'

Syd pressed a little harder on the accelerator, and Sandy reacted. 'What's going on? Have you heard feeding time at the zoo is nearly over, and you fear missing out?' Nic turned around to face them. 'Something like that, but brace yourself, guys. Sydney is about to do a driving manoeuvre.'

Sydney made space and changed lanes whilst the white car stayed in its lane. He checked the mirrors, gathered a little speed, and went to move back to the left as an exit was approaching, but a fast-moving cyclist had come into the gap.

Sandy shrieked. 'Bike'

The cyclist was oblivious to the car having changed lanes, but fortunately, Syd had eased off, so there was enough room for them both. 'Wow, now that was close. Who would ride a bike that fast in these suburban streets anyway?'

'It was probably one of the Armstrongs.'

'One of them, Rose?'

'Yes, either Lance Armstrong, avoiding his creditors after his doping fiasco, or Duncan Armstrong, the Australian swimmer, getting back on the bike after his health scare.'

Syd managed to weave across the left lane and took the exit, then slowed down and pulled to a stop. The white Camry passed them along the other road, but they were too far down their road to catch any other details.

They waited about ten minutes, and then Syd drove through the local streets, taking right-hand turns until they were back on the main thoroughfare. The white car was not in view.

They arrived at the Wildlife Reserve, paid the entry fare, and wandered around until late afternoon, looking at the animals and watching the other animals, watching the actual animals. Syd sipped on a coffee. 'It's refreshing to see the younger generation having such a good time, Mr Thyme.'

'Yes, Syd, it's a real children's paradise here.'

'I was referring to the three women with us.'

'Me too.' Nic walked over to them. 'Are you guys ready to go back to the ship?'

'Sure, we've even had matching Henna tattoos done to mark the occasion.'

'Oh wow, can I see them?'

Rose added. 'No, not unless you get one done too.'

They nodded to a display tent where the artist was, so Nic moved over and viewed the tattoos. The curtain was closed behind him, and Rose looked at the other two women and nodded. They stepped around to the back of the tent and watched as Nic was directed to a small couch to lie down for the procedure: *"Now, close your eyes sir, and please don't open them until I say so."*

About fifteen minutes later, the curtain parted, and Nic stepped out. Half his face was covered in a tattoo similar to the one Mike Tyson has over the left side of his head. Nic smiled and raised his hand. 'That was great, guys; I didn't feel a thing when she did this.' He showed them the delicate work on the back of his hand. 'She has done a great job. I even had a lovely face massage at the same time.' Rose, Sandy and Dee-Dee leaned forward and nodded. 'Nice.'

They moved towards the carpark and said nothing more along the way. Nic was either oblivious to the fact that there was a second tattoo on his face or was an outstanding actor. Rose and Sandy knew the latter was not the case and they finally laughed.

Nic looked at them. 'What's up, guys? Too much red cordial?'

Meanwhile, Syd had caught up to them and was chugging the last of a can of beer which he dropped the bottle into a rubbish bin. 'Hey Nic, what's with the Tribal tattoo on your face? Did you lose a bet or something?'

Nic brushed the right side of his face and shook his head. 'What are you talking about? She only did the back of my hand.' Dee-Dee pulled a compact mirror from her handbag and tossed it to him. Nic opened it and smiled.

'Damn you, Rose,' then he laughed. 'I know they're only temporary and will fade or can be washed off with some hard scrubbing. So, if I'm lucky, I won't have to see anyone for a few days. Oh, that's right, we have lunch with Carmel De Soto on Monday. I can always say I missed my flight. Maybe Rose can step in for me?'

Rose glanced at Sandy and was about to re-spond, but Syd spoke instead. 'It's only henna, Nic and will last about two weeks. Not like this one.' He removed his chauffeur cap, revealing a bald head and a skull tattoo. 'Yep, I thought doing this was so cool in my youth, but now I've got a head full of wrinkled prunes with two bloodshot eyes.'

They were all about to climb back into the car when Nic stopped. 'How many beers have you had, Syd?' Syd counted down on his fingers. 'Two. One with lunch, and that one I just finished. They were both light beers. Is there a problem?'

Nic nodded. 'Not really, but I should've said something earlier. I have a zero alcohol policy with any of my drivers. It just complicates things if there's an incident. The first thing the police say is, '*Have you been drinking, sir?*'. It's always easier to say 'no' than 'yes, but only light beer.'

Syd nodded. 'Fair enough, and sorry. Are you good to drive then?' Nic nodded, they swapped sides and drove them back to the ship.

'Yep, I've only had a couple of milkshakes, two ice creams and a bagful of peanuts that I pinched from the pouch of a wallaby.'

20

In the morning and after breakfast, they'd again managed to leave the ship and were waiting back in the apartments for Syd to arrive. Nic's phone chirped, and he nodded to the women that Syd had arrived, so they made their way downstairs.

Syd was standing next to his car rather than sitting inside and Nic knew this meant they needed to have a private conversation. Nic helped the others into the car. 'Jump in, guys, Syd and I need to have a quick chat.'

Syd and Nic moved along the footpath. 'What's up, Syd?'

'I had a visit last night from our friends in the white Toyota Camry. They followed me back to the car depot and approached me while waiting for my Uber.'

'Did anything happen?'

'Not really, apart from them thinking I was you. It was all bizarre. They kept calling me Mr Thyme, so I didn't correct them.' Syd suddenly stopped talking. 'Hey, I've just worked out why. I had removed my cap as my head was getting a little warm, and they would've seen the tattoo on my head. They must have been briefed that the man with the tattoo was Mr Thyme. So, unless they'd previously seen me without my cap, they wouldn't have known that I had one. You drove us back, so they must have assumed that I was you in the passenger seat.'

'I'm glad you got that confusion sorted, Syd. What did they say?'

'Back off, Mr Thyme, that sort of thing. Return home to Brisbane. We know you are staying on the ship. Don't stick your nose into stuff you know nothing about. That's about it.'

'Did you get a picture of them or anything?'

Syd looked at him and smiled. 'That was interesting too as they must have cased out the place beforehand. They knew where the on-site cameras were, as there was quite a bit of backward walking. They even leant into the car and snapped off my dash cam. I got the licence plate, and I've rung Chewy, and he hooked into the surveillance cameras from across the road. The two men won't bother us for at least a week or two. Something about having overstayed their VISA.'

'Not Aussies?'

Syd continued. 'Nope, most likely from New Zealand. They kept calling each other 'Bro' and talked about the All Blacks. I left it with Chewy, and he's just texted me to say the Department of Immigration is making an early visit to the boys.'

Nic grinned. 'Good work, I think we'd better lay low today. Let's return to the ship. I don't think the others will be disappointed as they have to get their heads around all the Aged Care stuff before the real party starts tomorrow.'

'OK mate, give me a call if you need anything. I might stay here for a while and help out the builder. I can do some of the basic electrical stuff.'

Nic nodded again. 'Thanks. I'll get the Courtesy Bus from the ship to collect us from here. Drive the car into one of the garages, leave it there overnight and take the Uber home once it is dark. You can camp here overnight if you want to.'

'Sure, I always keep a swag in the back of the car that way I can keep an eye on the coppers.'

'The police?'

'No mate, the copper piping is often stolen from work sites if the place is not secured properly.'

Nic grinned. 'I must be getting old, Syd. I didn't make that connection.'

'At least you're not as old as me. I've just turned sixty-five and the sum of three ex-wives, three children and three grandchildren. My eldest grand-child just got married, and they are expecting a little one. I'm too young to be a great-great-grand-father.'

Nic smiled, then went to the car's rear door, slid it open and sat inside, closing it behind him. 'Change of plans, guys. We're returning to the quay as we have to lay low. The ship will be the safest place.'

Rose had picked up on the seriousness of his tone. 'What's up, Nic? Is there anything we need to be aware of?'

'I'd prefer not to discuss it here, Rose. I'll get the boat bus to pick us up, and we'll spend the next couple of days on board, studying like doped-out university students for the big exam the next day.'

'Speak for yourself, Nic, I'm still a University student, doing my Honours.'

'Sorry Dee-Dee. I forgot it's my age, you know. I'm nearly forty.'

'It's a couple of years away, Nic and your birthday is not until next month.'

'Yep, I forgot that too.'

Rose and Sandy looked at her. 'So you know when it is Dee-Dee? Have you met his sisters too?'

'Of course, I know everything about him. I even know his real name.' Nic smiled again. 'Please don't go there Dee-Dee. I don't think you want to poke that bear.'

Rose and Sandy looked at her, then towards Nic, but Syd came to the car and opened the door. 'Time to go, kids, the boat bus is here. Have a good time, Mr Thyme, you too, Parsley, Sage, and Rosemary. I'll keep in touch.' Syd then walked to the front apartment and went up the stairs.

The shuttle bus pulled to a stop, and a flamboyantly dressed driver stepped down from it. He was about forty and dressed as a bright pink frill-neck lizard. 'I've heard a make-up emergency needs my magic fingers. Where is he?' He returned to the bus and extracted a very large make-up case. Rose pointed over to Nic. 'Over here, Mr Lizard, it's our Mr Nic that needs a little nip and tuck.'

'Oh my lord, Sweetie, what have they done?' He looked at Nic's tattooed face and softly turned it from side to side. 'I can only do the impossible; the miracles take a little longer. This will take more than I've brought, so it's back in the ship bus, boys and girls. Let's get back on board and into my secret laboratory. ASAP.'

The group took off, and Sandy called out to the driver. 'I'm sorry, Mr Lizard, is tonight's on-board stage performance from 'Priscilla, Queen of the Desert?'

'What makes you say that, Sweetie? Call me Lizzie, by the way.'

'Your outfit, isn't it from the '94 movie with Terrence Stamp and Guy Pearce?'

Lizzie called back. 'Oh no, this one is from 'Jurassic Park the Musical,' but we haven't quite worked out how a frill neck lizard manages to sing a duet with a dinosaur but throw a flouncy fluffy ruffle around the neck of anything, and they look scary enough.'

They were able to re-board without any trouble. Nic and the group were led down into the bowels of the ship and were now under the waterline. The lizard man kept going, and they finally came to a door that had a decal sticker on it: *'Be where the lizard bites. He says you taste better that way.'*

Lizzie stepped forward. 'In here, please. I've instructions to do a two-fer. I'll remove the tattoo and make one of you look like Thelma from the Simpsons.' He opened the door, and the four stepped into the small space. Nic showed him Rose's ID 'It's Velma from Scooby Doo, not Thelma from The Simpsons.'

'Oh my, which of you am I supposed to do the make-over for? The tattoo will come off with acetone and a loofah; it's only temporary. Although I like one on the back of your hand, that's a keeper. I can use my magic spray, and make it last longer than a few days. Do we have a deal?'

Nic nodded, and then Rose sighed and stepped forward. 'I'm the one to be Velma. I guess you need to cut and dye my hair?'

Lizzie looked at Rose and took her face softly in his hands. 'Nothing of the sort, Sweetie. I know people who would kill to have your beautiful elfin face and glorious auburn locks. Have you ever done any acting or modelling? What are you, an American size four?'

Rose smiled. 'Not quite, but Sandy and I used to run a couture shop in Brisbane, it was called 'The She Shed'. We closed it when they built the new road through Brett's Wharf.'

Lizzie looked at Rose and fluttered his hand at his face. 'Hang on, hang on. I've got a card somewhere here. I never forget a pretty face or a pretty place.' He picked up an old tin box, rummaged through it, pulled out a Rolodex and flicked through that until he reached the 'T's. 'As in this shop?'

They were all stunned.

'I went there once and clearly remember those two fine young ladies ran it. Rosie something and Sandra maybe? One of my crew had to get hold of a really special outfit, it was a fashion emergency. They were to be a witness for a marriage ceremony on board the ship, and we only had cash, but not enough. Those stupid card machine things weren't working either. It was during a scary Brisbane storm, and there was a power blackout, but they opened the doors anyway. We got the dress, shoes and a clutch for less than one hundred and fifty dollars cash. I think I've still got the receipt somewhere here.' Lizzie turned the card over, and the receipt had been sticky-taped to the back. He unstuck it and read it aloud. '$450.'

Rose nodded. 'Yes, that was indeed us.' Lizzie reached for his purse. 'I can settle the rest now if you're happy to take it.'

Rose shook her head. 'No, it's not necessary, but back to what you said about 'nothing of the sort', so you don't need to cut or dye my hair?'

'Look around Sweetie, you are in the presence of everything and anything to wear, whatever or whomever you desire to be. Are you supposed to be in disguise or something? This 'Velma' thing doesn't do you justice at all.'

Nic grinned. 'Yes, it's a disguise. We're on a mission to find something out, it's pretty big. Like 'Mr Big not marrying Carrie Bradshaw' big, but we can't talk about it here.'

Lizzie looked at Nic. 'Oh Sweetie, if only you weren't married. I bet all the clocks stopped on that day.' Rose shook her head. 'Oh no, he's not ma...'

Nic managed to dig Rose in the ribs before she could complete her sentence. 'Yes, I know. It's funny that most people get celebration cards at their wedding, but I also had a few that read, "What a waste." I even had a note left on one of them by the Marriage Celebrant, it read *"Call me if it doesn't work out..."*'

'Don't you hate it when that happens?'

The voice came from behind, it was Big Julie rejoining them.

Lizzie nodded towards Nic. 'Give me ten minutes with this handsome creature to remove the fake tattoo, but the 'Velma' thing may have to wait until later tonight. Are you OK with that, Rosa?' Rose nodded reluctantly and then Lizzie looked at Nic. 'Sit down here, and I'll start on your face.'

Ten minutes later, after scrubbing, rubbing and a tubbing of acetone, the fake tattoo was gone, and Nic's face was fresh and clean.

Lizzie was admiring his handiwork, then started to peel off his frill neck lizard's frill neck. 'It's four hours to show time so I need to get ready. Wouldn't it be lovely to live in a world of show tunes and dress up like Audrey Hepburn or Barbra Streisand?

Rose looked at him. 'Been there, done that. I did a six-week stint in a stage show called 'Fair Ladies' at the La Boite Theatre in Brisbane in my younger days.'

Lizzie fluttered his hands excitedly 'What do you mean? Can it be true? How, when, where? Tell me more, we always need an understudy for Eliza Doolittle.'

Rose shook her head. 'That's something else that happened long ago, too.'

Big Jule Julie then placed his massive paw on Nic's shoulder. 'Can I count on you as an understudy for the show too, Nic? We could use a tenor for the role of Freddy. I could do it, but I'm too tall. It looks funny having a towering Freddy on stage, singing lovey-dovey stuff to a five-foot-tall Eliza. I'm better left just doing the backup singing.'

Nic shrugged. 'Been there, but haven't done that.'

Rose looked at him. 'Been where?'

'I've been a Freddy and experienced unrequited love, but they say it never dies as it's just beaten down into a private place where it lies bitter and twisted.'

Rose shook her head. 'Oh, poor Nic, at least you have the troll under your bed.'

Lizzie then started to usher them toward the door. 'Out then, please. If you're not going to be in the show, I need to get ready.'

21

Nic's group returned to the promenade area to find which of the bars had opened early. Rose managed to break away and took comfort in a very cold, and very icy, early morning blue mock-martini. The others located her, sat down at a table and all stared at her colourful early morning heart starter.

Nic moved closer, dipped his finger into the blue liquid, and placed it into his mouth. 'It's only nine o'clock in the morning, how can you get into that already?'

Rose pulled her glass closer. 'Keep your not-so-well-manicured, furry fat fingers to yourself.'

'I've washed my hands this morning. Oh, hang on, it might have been last night after sharing the beer-nuts in the bar with Big Julie in the Casino.'

'That's disgusting.'

'Well, so is that blue dye they have put on your iced soda water to make it look like a martini.'

'Damn you, Nic.'

All this time, Dee-Dee had said nothing but finally broke her silence. 'Nic, when will we actually start on the thing we're here for?'

Nic shrugged and Dee-Dee continued: 'Anyway, I've done most of the prep work, and reviewed Sandy's notes. She'd picked up some stuff that I'd missed. It's a real insight into the world of State Government operations, but I've only ever done the paper theory so far.' Sandy nodded. 'Thanks, Dee-Dee.'

Dee-Dee's phone rang and she moved away. About ten minutes later Dee-Dee returned. 'That was Seiko. She's been visiting a few Aged Care centres around Brisbane and found something interesting at one out at Redcliffe. It was supposed to be a fully operational centre, but she only found five mouldy bins out the back.'

Nic motioned for the group to find a more private area, and they sat down again. 'I'll get Chewy to find out who operates it. Did she find anything else?'

'Only that the bins had a logo on them, it read 'GOT Rubbish?' She'd seen the same logo at another Aged Care Centre two days prior. That centre was still operating, but when she tried to take a photo of the bin at that centre, a couple of heavies came from nowhere and tried to take her phone from her. She eventually had to flash her Police ID to make them settle down.'

Nic nodded. 'Good to know she can handle herself, but I hope that doesn't come back to our investigation. We might have to speed things up a little. I'll give Carmel a ring and tell her Sandy, and I managed to get an earlier flight and that we've already arrived. Perhaps we can meet today instead of lunch on Monday.'

Rose let out a breath. 'That sounds like a better plan than listening to you warble on a stage. Anyway, I think I've torn muscle in my leg climbing all the stairs around here.'

Nic looked at her. 'At least try and hide your disappointment, Rose. After all, your pain is lame when you fake a sprain.' Nic then looked at Big Julie. 'Would it be OK if we skipped the show and did some real work?'

'Sure, whatever floats your boat. The show must go on as they say.'

They all stood up, and Big Julie moved over to a wall phone to call Lizzie to let him know Nic's group had bailed on the show. Big Julie lowered the phone.

'Are you sure you're out too, Nic? Lizzie was in the middle of putting together a My Fair Lady outfit, especially for you. There were sequins and everything.'

Nic shook his head. 'Freddy Eynsford-Hill may have been a wimp, but he certainly didn't wear sequins. He sang about lost love on the street where you live.'

Nic began to sign the line from the song. "On the street where you live." Rose looked at him. 'Please stop. Leave it for those that sing it well.' Nic continued to sing the melody: '*I feel I've missed my calling and should have been on stage.*'

Big Julie laughed. 'Just how long have you guys been doing all of this scam investigations stuff with Nic?'

Nic stopped singing. 'With Rose and Sandy, it's been about eighteen months, but Dee-Dee has been with me for four years.'

Big Julie grinned. 'Did they retire from the police force and come to work for you?'

'Nup, nothing like that. I'm just a regular Charlie, and they are my three Angels.'

Rose piped up. 'Yes, he's Charlie Brown, and we keep pulling the football away from him every time he tries to take a kick. We are all his Lucy.'

'That's funny, Rose. Have you ever thought of doing stand-up comedy? We have an open-mike night here on Wednesdays.'

'No thanks, I think I'll retire before the tall poppy syndrome takes me down.'

'So, have you done stand-up as well as stage performing?'

'No, just being around Nic for the last eighteen months has been all the funny stuff that I need.' Nic grinned. 'Wow, thanks, Rose.'

Rose was quick to retort. 'That's funny peculiar, Nic, not funny, ha-ha.'

Nic stretched. 'You know, I could get used to living on a big ship and not having a care in the world. The meal times are regular, and the choice of drinks is amazing.'

Rose sighed. 'What about the mountainous seas and the inevitable iceberg?'

'Rose, they have sonars that pick up anything bigger than an iceberg lettuce.'

'Well, what about the inevitable stranding on a deserted island, like that guy who played Forrest Gump?'

'Gee, you are a doomsayer this morning.'

'Well, you were the one that wanted me to don the Eliza Doolittle stuff. I'm more of Holly Go-lightly girl anyway.'

They looked at her. 'You know from the 1962 film, 'Buy my ring at Tiffany's.''

'It was 'Breakfast at Tiffany's, Rose.'

'I know, I just wanted to know if you were listening. It's my favourite film. I sang 'Moon River' in the stage show too.'

Big Julie piped up. 'That song wasn't in My Fair Lady.' Rose continued. 'We made it up as we went along. I even sang wonderful, S marvellous' on one occasion too. It's from 'Funny Face' with Audrey and Fred, now that was an age difference; he was sixty, and she wasn't even a flirty thirty.'

Nic grinned. 'Anyway, whilst we're all here, I'll call Chewy and see if he's found out anything else.' Nic called via Zoom and put the phone on the coffee table with the speaker on. It was answered immediately. 'Yo Nic, how is the Scooby gang? You're looking good, but what happened to the Mike Tyson face tattoo?'

'I had it surgically removed, along with half my face. I can only tell bare-faced lies now and not be two-faced about it.'

'Hey, that was Funny Face.'

The trio of women looked at each other, but Sandy piped up first. 'Were you listening in on our private conversation? Rose was just talking about Fred and Audrey in the film.'

'Well, I am Nic, 'Batman' Thorns', psychic sidekick.'

Nic nodded. 'Ok then, my Red, Red Robin that comes bob, bob, bobbing along, what have you found out? Has Seiko been in touch?'

'Yes, and she's sent me photos to work on. The 'GOT Rubbish' on the bins is still a mystery. It looks like an old logo. I also found an old, registered business name, but there weren't any details about the previous proprietor. The Aged Care Minister, Paul Roberts, D.O.B, 13 September 1954, seems to check out. He's squeaky clean, almost too clean. The details of the other guy, Phillip Joffrey Robertson, D.O.B 14 October 1978, are a little more sketchy. He's supposed to have a Master of Business Administration from the Bond University on the Gold Coast, but I can't find any record of his name there.'

Sandy laughed, 'His middle name is Joffrey?'

Rose interjected. 'Maybe, but they could have been 'Game of Thrones fans, A bit early, though, as the series only started in 2011.'

Nic shook his head. 'Rose, what's that got to do with Joffrey?'

'Joffrey was the child King that had Sean Bean beheaded.' They all looked at her. 'Yes, that was the one show my parents allowed me to watch. My Father wanted to align himself with a quest for world domination. I thought the show was a bit stark until my brother and I realised we could call Father 'Jamie' and Mother 'Cersei'. We try to get away with it even now.'

Chewy responded. 'OK, thanks for that. I hadn't even gone down that track, but nothing means nothing until it means something, doesn't it, Nic?'

'So true, my little caped crusader.'

The call was disconnected, Big Julie left the room, and the group went to the dining hall for lunch, and to quench their thirst.

They decided to watch the matinee performance of 'My Fair Lady'. Sandy and Nic were in fine voice, but Rose refused to partake in the frivolities. The actors playing Eliza and Freddy actually left the stage in the middle of the performance and reminded the audience they were the show's stars, but were happy to take anyone back up on stage with them if anybody wanted to keep singing.

The closing numbers included Freddy doing an impromptu version of 'Putting on the Ritz', including a tap-dancing routine. Rose whispered to no one in particular. 'That song was not in the original play or the movie.'

Nic stood and started to move along the aisle. Rose assumed he was heading for the stage and held out her hand to stop him. 'Nic, remember you're supposed to keep a low profile, even if it is on a cruise ship in the middle of the ocean.'

Nic sat back down. 'We're not at sea, Rose.'

'Nope, but if you blow your cover, we'll all be at sea anyway. Sit down, stop singing and behave.'

'Damn, you, Eliza Doo-too-much, not Eliza Doolittle.'

22

The small audience called for an encore, so the troupe complied with another song from another musical. Lizzie took centre stage, dressed in a lizard outfit, and did a very campy version of 'The Love Boat' theme to close the show.

Nic started to stand and leaned into Rose. 'This is crazy, everybody is singing now...*please* Rose....'

'No, remember where you are and who you are. You are Nic 'Batman' Thorn, and I've never heard Bruce Wayne warbling whilst fighting his crimes in Gotham City. Stop trying to impress the crowd, besides, what if Carmel De Soto is here somewhere?'

Nic slumped down in his chair. 'This is the first and last time we go cruising together, Rose.'

'The ship hasn't left the port, Nic, so don't get my hopes up. We should have an early night and study the Aged Care reports. We need tomorrow to get ready for Monday.'

Nic nodded. 'OK, let's go. I still have to make that call to Carmel. So are we heading to the dining room or back to the cabins for room service?'

'To the cabins, Nic; after all, tomorrow is only a day away.'

Nic looked at Rose. 'Don't you dare, That's a song lyric from "Annie," and it doesn't belong in 'My Fair Lady." Nic hummed the melody back to the cabin.

They gathered in Nic's cabin, ordered room service and began reviewing the Aged Care reports. Nic's phone rang. It was Chewy.

'Thanks for the tip about Joffrey, Rose. I checked out Phillip's Facebook and Instagram sites. The guy is a huge Game of Thrones fan, and there is some chatter that he's trying to organise a trip to Iceland, where they filmed the series. Some people need to get a better hobby, as there are so many great sites to visit from the Star Wars films. So, don't get me started on the Game of Thrones stuff.'

Nic added. 'OK, do what you can. I'll let Carmel know that Sandy and I have arrived early, and we can meet up tomorrow instead of Monday. We won't be working in the office, apart from Dee-Dee. Carmel hasn't mentioned the third person that will be in the office, though.'

Rose stood up. 'I've had a big day and will call it a night.'

Nic nodded. 'OK, but it's just after eight. Haven't you forgotten something?'

Rose looked around. 'Nope, I don't think so,' and was startled as there was a knock at the door. Nic called out. 'Please come in. Rose has been eagerly waiting for her makeover to become the wonderful Rosa Giardino.'

Rose looked at Lizzie, still dressed as a Frill Neck lizard and he had in tow a pile of makeup cases. Lizzie led Rose to a bedroom and shut the door behind him.

The others overheard his first comment. 'Sweetie, this will be much worse for me than you. Please keep still.'

Rose claimed .'Hey, I'm the one that will end up looking like a cartoon character, and not in a good way.'

'Not true, Sweetie. I'm used to dressing people up, not down. Do you know if there is anything worth drinking in the bar fridge?'

'For me or you?' Rose moved over, opened the bedroom bar fridge, and held up two bottles of vodka. 'Just enough for me. I think you need to be sober for whatever you're about to do to me.'

'OK, Sweetie, firstly, a couple of things. I will have to cut your hair into the bob style. I couldn't come up with a wig I could shape, The second thing is, well, if I make you up now, you won't be able to sleep on it. Can you sleep standing up?'

'No, I don't think I'm a horse. Any other options?.'

'I could follow you around as your personal attaché.'

'Nic already does that for me.' There was a muffled laugh from the outside of the door. 'I heard that, Rosa.' Lizzie continued. 'Sweetie, you are pretty, aren't you? I won't be able to disguise your retrousse nose unless you want a prosthetic one.'

'Nope, it's all good, Lizzie. Just do the hair, makeup, dress, and the.....I give up, then. Double damn you, Nic.'

Nic called out from the other side of the door. 'Hey, I heard that too, Rosa.'

After about forty minutes, the bedroom door opened, and Rosa Giardino stepped out dressed in a short red pleated skirt, baggy orange turtle neck jumper, long socks, and Mary-Jane shoes.

Rose looked at the others. 'Jinkies, where's Scooby Doo gone?'

Nic drew a pair of black-rimmed glasses from his trouser pocket, placed them on Rose's face, and stepped back to admire the work. He smiled. 'Bellissimo.' Lizzie had followed her out and started softly clapping. 'This is some of my best work. I think I will cry. She is beautiful, in a down-to-earth, dowdy, girl-next-door, and super-hero sort of way.' Rose sighed. 'Velma is not a superhero. She just works with a good-looking hunky guy, a stunning blonde mystery solver, a doped-out hungry dude, and a big Maine Coon cat.'

'Scooby-Doo was a dog, Sweetie, and I think Daphne was a redhead.'

'I was talking about us.'

Nic nodded, 'Hey, that's the first time you've said I'm a good-looking, hunky guy.' Rose looked at him. 'Big Julie is the hunk, you're the doped-out hungry dude.' Nic grinned. 'Thanks, Rosa. Ok, by the way, your hair looks great.'

Nic held up his phone and showed them the photo ID they hoped to match. It was a good comparison. 'Thanks, Lizzie, good job. It's a pity that Carmel won't meet Rosa tomorrow.'

Rose looked at him suspiciously. 'Why?'

'She rang when you were getting all 'Velma'd' up and said that she has to return to Brisbane first thing Monday morning. It seems the case of the dodgy Aged Care centre invoicing scam thing has had some light shone upon it, and it is all about to get in the open.'

'Damn you, Nic, Can I take this off then?'

Lizzie shook his head, 'Sorry, Sweetie; it won't come off for at least five days. It's my special stuff, and you wouldn't want to see what I look like without my makeup.'

Nic smiled. 'I know, what a shame, but we can still go on our own Scooby-Doo mystery in Brisbane. Dee-Dee will stay down here to finish the renovations at the apartments.'

Sandy piped up. 'Well, if Rose is dressed up as Velma, can I at least pretend to be Daphne? I'll have to dye my hair red, though.' Sandy then looked over at Nic, 'What about you? Have you ever thought of being a dirty blonde?'

Nic laughed, then realised Sandy referred to the character 'Shaggy' rather than the white-dyed-haired Fred Jones. 'Sorry, Sandy. I'm more of a devilishly handsome super-sleuth, solving scams and frauds in pursuit of justice and the Milky Way.'

Lizzie looked at him. 'Sweetie, it would only take me five minutes. I can glue a scruffy beard on you, but you'll have to work on the dopey character look yourself.'

Rose laughed. 'He won't need help.'

There was a second knock, the door opened and Rose jumped. 'Who could that be at this hour? Scooby-Doo himself?' Big Julie stepped in. 'Yo, it's me, guys; I wondered how the....Wow, our super-sleuth, Velma Dinkley, is in the house. I'm sure I can come up with a mystery for you to solve. Let me think. How about the sinking of the Titanic? Or the mystery of The Bermuda Triangle?'

Rose nodded. 'I've got a mystery straight up. How did you unlock the door?'

Big Julie held his wrist up, and it had a small black plastic square similar to the one Nic was wearing. 'We are trailing these on board at the moment. They're a great invention, all thanks to Chewy and Nic. I think it's called "IVY" and saves us from carrying around keys and access cards.' Big Julie waved his forearm around, making noises like it was a Jedi Knight light sabre. 'Swoosh, brr swoosh.'

Rose rolled her eyes. 'What's that supposed to be?'

Nic nodded. 'Well, us men, when we were doing our men things, with those things, we have to make sure we're making the right noises.' Nic then sighed. 'Well, Big Julie, this is where we'll say our goodbyes.'

Big Julie nodded. 'What so soon? We didn't even get you guys up on stage.'

Rose responded. 'I know; I was so looking forward to it too.'

Nic looked over at Rose. 'You know that we don't just investigate scams on dry land; there is such a thing as high treason on the high seas.'

Lizzie clamped his hands. 'And now I know where to get someone to play Eliza Doolittle at short notice. Sweetie, we would love to have you on board, and anyone that's part of the troupe can stay and play for free.'

'Er...I'm a good girl, I am.'

They laughed, and Nic took back control of the conversation. 'OK, we'll do breakfast, then head back to the apartments to check on the renovations.'

Dee-Dee quietly interrupted them. 'The bathrooms are finished, and I've been talking to the tiler. The kitchens are almost finished too. I'll stay there tomorrow if you guys want to catch a plane to Brisbane.'

'Have you heard anything more from Seiko?'

Sandy looked at him. 'I thought she was supposed to be keeping you up to date.'

'Yes, but I'm good with that. I don't want to get in between two sisters. I have enough of that between Nic and Sassy.' Rose and Sandy looked at each other. 'OMG, your twin sister's name is Sassy? Quick, hand me a phone and I will google 'Sassy@Murrayville'.'

Nic smiled. 'Go your hardest, Sandy; it's what we call her, not her name.'

Rose sighed. 'That doesn't make sense, Nic. She's either 'Sassy' or sassy. I think it means bold and spirited, and it makes sense she'd be your twin.'

'Yep, that describes me to a T.'

'We were talking about Sassy.'

'OK, but who is she again, Rose?'

'Your sister...'

Nic shook his head. 'I don't have a sister called Sassy.' and he began ushering everyone out of his room. 'I've got to get some beauty sleep and will see you at breakfast at nine a.m. sharp.'

'But Nic...we want to call your sister and introduce ourselves.'

'I don't know her number either.'

It was well after 9.30 and Nic was late for breakfast, so they were worried as it was so unlike him. Dee-Dee wasn't there either. Sandy looked at Rose. 'Have you tried ringing him? Besides, where can you go if you're on a ship?'

'I don't know. He could have jumped overboard as you were pretty hard on him last night trying to work out his sister's name.'

'Nope, I think it's something else. Maybe the real Batman wants his suit back?' Rose was about to call when Big Julie approached them, and he wasn't happy. 'Nic has bailed on us. He took the red-eye back to Brisbane and left you guys with the bill.'

Rose nodded. 'He wouldn't have done that without telling us, and where's Dee-Dee? Hang on; we're supposed to be staying here for free.'

'Oh, yeah, I forgot. Anyway, Dee-Dee has gone back to the apartments already as the workers jackhammered into a water pipe, and it's now a soggy mess. She's helping them clean things up. Did you check your phones?'

Rose and Sandy looked at their phones, and both Nic and Dee-Dee had left an SMS message. Sandy piped up. 'How rude; I would have thought they could have rung us. They know we're on holiday and not looking at our phones.'

23

Big Julie nodded. 'Well, they rang me instead. They told me to let you guys know and to tell you to stop turning your phones face down at night. The blue light phone thing is a myth; the only thing that makes you look older is growing older.'

Rose nodded. 'So, why are you looking so grumpy?'

'Sunday is my non-work day, and I like to sleep in until at least ten, then go for a five-kilometre run around the block.'

Rose shook her head. 'We're on a ship, so there's not around the block, it's a circle of about two hundred metres.'

Big Julie nodded. 'My life goes around in circles. Sometimes, I run so fast that I catch up with my-self. Besides, it's my day off, so I can do what I like, and now I can't.'

Rose nodded. 'Sorry about that. Can we make it up to you somehow?'

'OK, I guess you might be able to. The Archies are being set up in the Sydney Gallery, and my wife has a portrait on display. Do you think you could smuggle me off the ship?'

'Why do we need to smuggle you off-board? You're the Cruise Director; surely you have the power to direct or miss-direct the staff, as the case may be?'

'Not quite. I'm not supposed to leave the ship in case something happens. If one of you stays in my room, we can pretend that I'm quarantined in quarters, that way I might be able to sneak off for a couple of hours.'

Sandy grinned. 'OK, that makes sense, but how will you sneak off? You're two metres tall, and I didn't see a Big Bird costume in Lizzie's costume cabin.'

'Nope, but if I put on a Basketball Uniform. You two could get dressed as cheerleaders, so that might work.'

Rose looked at him. 'Are you serious?'

'Yes, or I could just jump off the back and start swimming with sharks.'

'Come on, Big Julie. Go old school and ask the Captain if you could have a few hours off.'

'That might work too.'

They finished breakfast, went back to their cabins, completed packing, and met with Big Julie on the gangway level. This time, he was smiling. 'You know the Captain's quite a nice guy.'

Sandy smiled. 'So, he said yes?'

'And he told me to have the rest of the day off. There was one condition, I had to try to convince Rose to stay onboard and star in 'My Fair Lady.''

Rose shook her head. 'Not going to happen. I think I make a better Velma.'

'So, I can't convince you then?' Big Julie sighed. 'Oh well, at least I tried. So let's enjoy my day off. I'd love you guys to meet my wife.'

They disembarked and walked through the Royal Botanic Gardens up to the gallery. Big Julie's wife was waiting for them on the front steps, she had lanyards for them, and a guard was with her.

'Hi, I'm Mackenzie, but call me Mac. Pleased to meet you.' She then gave Jules a quick peck on the cheek. 'Oh, and this is Art; he will be our guide.'

The man nodded, and Rose looked at him. 'Hey Art, do you get to hang around on all the gallery walls?' Art looked at her. 'I've heard that before, Miss Represent. It wasn't funny the first time either.'

'My name is Miss Hinkley, not Miss Represent.'

'Oh, sorry. With that bob hair-do, you do represent someone else.'

Mac handed over the lanyards, and they stepped into the foyer. Other groups were waiting in line to go through, so Sandy looked around and noticed a poster for an upcoming exhibition. It was called 'Water'. 'Rose, I think you need to see this.' Sandy directed her to the poster.

Rose sighed. 'Damn you, Nic, I'm not pirouetting through another waterfall.'

Big Julie pulled up a link on his phone and showed it to Art, and he nodded. 'I've heard about this. The guys at GOMA in Brisbane thought the age of a tapestry was suspect, so called in a group to take some cuttings. It turned out it was all legitimate and was just a trial to test their security systems.'

'Yes, that was me before I became Velma.'

The guard nodded. 'Good job. Did you know your mascara was running at you looked like a panda?' Rose shrugged. 'I've heard that before too.'

Their allocated time for viewing arrived, and the group made the way through the portraits, finally arriving at the one Mac had painted of Big Julie. It was a total frontal nude, standing well over two metres high, but his face distorted as his head was encased in a large glass jar.

They moved along after making sure they had selected the portrait for at least a Packing Prize nomination and, about two hours later, were back in the front foyer saying their goodbyes to Mac and Art. A woman dashed through them, and they did their best to avoid her, but Rose was elbowed in her arm. *'I'm so sorry; I'm late. I hate being late. Oh good, I made it just in the nick of time.'*

Rose stared at her back as she disappeared into the waiting crowd of the gallery. 'She looks like someone we know from somewhere.'

The group returned to the ship and sat in a cafe. The drinks arrived, and Big Julie was still grinning. 'You know, guys, I think I should go AWOL more often. This was a good idea.'

Rose was about to respond when her phone rang. It was Chewy and Rose turned the speaker on. He blurted out. 'Have you heard from Nic? He's gone AWOL.'

Rose looked over to Big Julie. 'How does Chewy do that? He must be listening somehow.'

Big Julie waved his forearm at her. 'Swoosh, swoosh.' His phone then chirped as a message had arrived; he read it, peeled the small black 'watch' from his forearm, placed it in Rose's hand and held his finger to his lips. 'Sshh.'

Rose put it in her pocket, and they listened as Chewy continued: 'I've booked two flights back to Brisbane. You depart in about two hours. Can you get to the airport? The Aged Care fraud made the news, but that's not the worst of it.'

Rose nodded. 'Sure, we can do that, but what's the connection with us?'

Chewy hesitated. 'Nic's headshot is on the Courier Mail's newsfeed website.'

Big Julie arranged to have their luggage collected from the cabins and they were waiting in the departure area to be collected. A black Ford Transit van pulled into the collection area, and Syd called out from the driver's seat: 'Hop in the back. We've got some work to do.'

Big Julie stepped forward and moved around to the driver's seat whilst Syd went through the gap in the front seats to sit in the back. Rose and Sandy opened the rear doors and climbed in. Syd was sitting beside a large plastic tub, it was empty. Sandy looked at him, then to the tub. 'What's with the tub in the back seat?'

Syd chortled. 'Hey, that's not nice. I'm cuddly, not tubby.'

Rose sighed. 'She's talking about the plastic bucket. What's going on?'

'Well, I've just been updated about the Aged Care thing, and we need to make sure you are safe to go back into Brisbane.'

Rose nodded nervously. 'Do we have to get covered in invisible paint? Is that why the tub looks empty?'

'No, I've got to make sure your Velma look is sharp, and as for Sandy, I've got about fifteen minutes to turn her into a redhead, and the glamorous genuine Scooby-Doo gal that is Daphne.'

They sat down on the bench seats in the car, and Big Julie drove off for the airport. Sandy looked at Syd. 'This is ridiculous. I don't want to look like a cartoon character. Oops, sorry, Rose.'

Syd poured dye into the bucket. 'Have you seen the Courier Mail newsfeed?'

Rose shook her head. 'Nope.

'Google it on your phone.'

They did, but they couldn't find any reference or pictures of Nic. 'What are we supposed to be looking for?'

'Nic.'

Sandy responded. 'There's nothing here but rugby news. It's something about someone that's done something to someone, instead of being somewhere where they should have been, doing something to someone else they were supposed to be doing.'

Rose looked at her. 'Wow, that's real Nic Thorn gobble-de-gook. Good job.'

Sandy shrugged. 'Thanks, I'm learning from the best. Anyhow, Syd, why is Nic insisting we have to be disguised?'

'The Aged Care thing has hit the online pages, and apparently, the State Opposition leader will call a press conference at six o'clock tonight. He has made a claim about the shenanigans of the Aged Care Minister under "Parliamentary Privilege," and that's why you two have got to get back

ASAP. They can't suspect you are part of the Nic Thorn and Associates team looking into the fraud.'

Rose looked at him. 'Who are they?'

'They are them. They don't want you to know that we, as you and us, are looking into them, doing what they are not supposed to.'

'Could you write that down, Syd? You lost me at the first word.'

'Sorry, Rose, it was a one-time only, gobble-de-gooky statement, and if we can't see Nic, it means that Chewy's super Nic Thorn internet eraser wipey thing must work. Pretty impressive, I'd say.' Rose grinned. 'Or, the headline story has already moved on from the Aged Care thing.'

Syd nodded. 'Let's go with that.'

24

Sandy was now lying across the floor with her head leaning into the tub of red hair dye and Syd began to apply the red slurry. 'This won't take long, but you'll have to wear a shower cap on the flight back to Brisbane to ensure the dye sets.'

Sandy shook her head slowly. 'I need my head read for doing this.'

'That's funny, but please don't move. I don't want any of the dye running down your face, as you might look like a red panda. Your turn now, Rose.'

'Why? What do you have to do to me? I've already got the comic book look.'

Syd grinned. 'Please give me the watch and hold out your arm.' Rose pulled the watch from her pocket and handed it over. Syd then pulled a syringe gun from another pack. 'Don't worry; I'm also a Certified Safety Officer on construction sites.' Rose looked at the syringe. 'What are you going to do with that?'

Syd held the syringe to her arm, and it shot a tiny dot under the skin. 'Now hold the black 'watch' square to it, please.' Rose did, and it stuck fast.

'You now have a five thousand dollar piece of equipment on you. Please take good care of it, so says Nic.'

About twenty minutes later, Rose and Sandy stepped out of the back of the van, had changed their clothes and their disguises were down pat. Syd hugged them, and Big Julie saluted. 'Remember, if anyone asks, you are Rosa Giardino or Velma Hinkley it doesn't matter which one, and Sandy is Daphne De Maudlin.'

Syd handed over the plane tickets. There were no names on them.

Sandy nodded. 'Hey, Daphne De Maurier is a real person. She was an English novelist. Do I have to have an English accent then?'

Syd nodded. 'Not quite the same name, anyway she died about thirty years ago.'

Sandy nodded. 'Wow, it's no wonder I'm confused. I was supposed to be Sandra Bulloch when I arrived in Sydney, and now I'm leaving, I'm someone else.'

Syd helped them with their luggage, waved them off and Sandy used a scarf from her luggage over the shower cap. 'That's better; at least no one will wonder about wearing a tea cosy on my head.'

They checked in, went straight to the lounge, and sat down exhausted.

Rose leaned back in the lounge chair. 'I wonder what's happened to Nic? Maybe they found him hiding in the Bat cave?'

Flight QF536 to Brisbane is boarding; please go to the gate.

Rose's seat was S32, near the back of the plane and Sandy's was in M19. 'Hey, we're not together or flying Business Class. Damn you, Nic, or whatever your name is now.'

A steward handed Rose and Sandy each a sealed envelope as they boarded. A name was typed on each; it read 'Velma', and the other 'Daphne', and both were marked '***EAR***.'

The envelopes contained a mobile phone. They headed for their allocated seats, and fortunately, as the other passengers were not all aboard, were able to open their envelopes without others watching.

Rose carefully tore the top off hers, and it contained a printed email: *Velma, sorry to have left you so quickly. I had to get back to Brisbane to take control of things before things got out of control. There has been a significant change of direction in the investigation. All is not well in the house of Queensland Health. They are looking for a patsy, and it could be me. Keep safe, and keep invisible. EAR, with lots of P & S. Shaggy.'*

Rose wondered if it was the same note in both envelopes, then noticed that Sandy had stood up from her seat and appeared to be putting something away in the overhead locker. Their eyes met, so Rose held her hands and mouthed the words 'What the?' Sandy didn't respond.

Rose sat down and took out the phone. It was an old Nokia. Three numbers were stuck to the back of the phone, so assuming the top number was for hers, Rose texted the second one: '?' It came back '$\sqrt{}$'.

Rose considered texting the third number but was interrupted by the other passengers wanting to take their seats. It was too late by then anyway as they began to taxi for take-off.

The normal flight time was one and a half hours, and they were collecting their luggage at the carousel when their phones chimed.

The message read: *'Keep apart; you don't know each other.'*

Rose and Sandy separated and made their way towards the exits.

Rose noticed a driver holding a sign, 'Rosa G or Velma H', so she made her way over to the woman. 'I'm Rosa G.' The woman looked at her, nodded subtly, and held out as if to shake her hand, but instead moved her open palm over Rose's forearm. The watch lit up momentarily.

The woman nodded again. 'I am here to collect you.'

The driver took her luggage, and they walked towards the limousine area where a black Chrysler 300C was parked. Rose recognised it as one that Nic had used previously and felt a sense of relief. 'Where are we going?'

The driver drove off and kept looking straight ahead, 'To Nic's place.'

Sandy hadn't been collected and continued through the exit sliding doors and was waiting at the taxi stand. A yellow cab pulled to a stop, and the driver stepped out. 'Are you Daphne? Shaggy has sent me to collect you.'

Sandy looked at her. 'Yes, I am. How is Shaggy?'

The driver shook her head. 'Not here, get in the car, please.'

They exited the airport precinct and headed toward the city via Airport Link. As they approached Coronation Drive, the driver took the exit to the right instead of going straight over the Go-Between Bridge.

Sandy knew then she wasn't going home to West End.

The driver motored west for a couple of minutes, then turned into Park Road and pulled into a driveway at a small, high-set Queenslander. The property was rented by her friends, they were members of the jazz band 'The Sweetened Plums'

The lead singer Carly, and the drummer Sticks Out were waiting for her in the front garden. Sandy stepped out of the car, and Carly hugged her. 'Hello, Daphne,' then quickly led her inside the house.

Two other band members were in the kitchen, and in the middle of the table was another envelope addressed to 'Daphne'. Sandy sat down, took a deep breath, and stared at the envelope. 'So you guys are in on this too?'

Sticks Out shook his head and, in his best Hogan's Hero's 'Sergeant Schultz' impression, uttered the classic line 'I know nothing.' The band members stood and walked out of the room, leaving Sandy alone.

Sandy opened the envelope and inside was another email from Nic. This one went into more detail about the risks that they were now facing: *Dearest Daphne, congratulations. You are now a new backup singer for 'The Sweetened Plums'. Take care of yourself and keep safe. I don't know when, where, how or what we are implicated in. Limit your time outside for the moment. The band doesn't know anything about anything other than you could be in danger. EAR. Shaggy.'*

Sandy sighed. 'So, are we rehearsing? Daphne is here, and we need to get her into the groove. I've got to prove that I am worthy.'

Sticks laughed. 'That's not quite the lyrics, Daphne, but mixing Madonna songs into our jazz repertoire might be something we can work on.' He started a paradiddle on the side of the kitchen table.

'Thanks, and I'm glad you haven't had your ears pinned back.'

'Nope, Sticks Out. I've still got my ears that stick out.' He then tapped at his ears with the drumsticks. 'Ow, that hurts.' Carly stepped up and rubbed Sandy's shoulders. 'Do you know anything about what is happening? I got a text from Nic saying: *'I need a favour; I've arranged a new band member for you. Please look after her. Her name is Daphne. You might know her.'*

Sandy shook her head. 'I've no idea, but thanks for doing this, Carly.' Carly continued. 'Well, the two other guys weren't too happy about being told we were getting a new member, so we took a vote. Sticks and I voted 'yes', and Angus and Fungus voted 'no'. That means you have the casting vote, Daphne.'

Sandy nodded. 'I vote yes. So, let's work on some songs and see how we gel.'

The group headed downstairs to a band rehearsal area: soundproofing surrounded the walls and ceilings, and microphones and a recording desk were in a glass booth at the back of the room. Sticks sat behind his drum kit, Carly stood by the keyboard, and the other two picked up their guitars. Sandy looked around for her space, and Carly nodded to the booth. 'You're in there. Have you worked a sound desk before?'

'Not for a while. So Daphne, the newest band member, also does the sound?'

Carly grinned. 'Yes, but you can do the lighting too.' Sticks laughed. 'We have to keep you safe and invisible. If you turn the light off, it will go dark there, and no one will see you.'

Sandy grinned. 'Wow, I'm working a recording desk, the lighting, and being invisible. I get to multi-task.'

25

Meanwhile, Rose's driver had taken a different route from the airport to the city along Kingsford Smith Drive, and they passed the Brett's Wharf ferry stop area where 'The She Shed' used to be. Rose looked over to the driver and was about to say something when her Nokia phone chimed. '*P.S. Velma, you're not going to Southbank.*'

They joined the Inner City By-Pass, then took the exit into the Clem Seven tunnel, and about fifteen minutes later merged onto the M1 Motorway heading south towards the Gold Coast. Rose was staring out the passenger window and realised the driver had not yet told her where they were going.

'Excuse me; you said we were going to Nic's place at Southbank? I think you missed the turnoff about twenty minutes ago.'

The driver replied. 'Wow, you are very observant, aren't you?'

'Where are we going?'

'To Nic's place.'

Rose whispered, 'Damn you, Nic,' and she looked down at the phone, then decided to send a message off to Sandy: 'R.U.O.K?' and there was a prompt response: '*Remember Chicago and all that jazz.*'

Rose considered the comment and realised Sandy had referenced her jazz band friends, and knew they would protect her from any threat, as they were not just ordinary musicians, they were jazz musicians.

Rose sensed the driver was speeding, but at least they were in the fast lane. 'Do you know where you're going?'

'Yes.' And with that, the driver glanced in the rear vision mirror, took a quick look over her left shoulder and zipped across the five lanes into the Sanctuary Cove exit. 'To Nic's place.'

Rose held on for dear life. 'You don't usually work for Nic, do you?'

'No, I'm a transporter, and you're the parcel. Why couldn't I be working for him?' Rose sighed. 'You've been speeding, and he doesn't like drawing attention to us.' The driver grunted and pulled the car to a dusty stop. 'Oh, sorry for that, Miss Nanny-Pants. I was told to deliver to you by five thirty, and we are now here.'

Rose stepped out, took her luggage from the rear seat, and looked at the house, but before she could ask the driver where she was, the car was gone. The house was behind a two-metre-high brick fence, the double gates were shut and there was a large 'For Sale' sign on the front lawn. Rose was considering ringing Nic when a car door shut behind her. She hadn't noticed a car parked there when she arrived, so didn't turn around.

'Rosa? Rosa Giardino? Velma Hinkley? Is that you?' It was a man's voice, and she didn't recognise it, so she kept facing the house. The voice continued: 'I was sent to help you. Didn't you check your phone?'

Rose considered the reply but cautiously assumed it was a genuine directive, so opened her phone, and there was a message: *Uncle Grumpy-Pants will meet you there.* Rose smiled, then turned around, 'Damn you, Nic.'

The man walked closer and held out his hand. 'Hi, Rose/Rosa/Velma. Uncle Grumpy Pants, we meet again. This time, though, it's not to deliver a car to me, I'm here to protect you from whatever this is.' Rose looked at him, trying to determine if there was any family resemblance to Nic, but decided there wasn't. 'So, how do we get in?'

'Hold that plastic square on your arm over the gate lock.' Rose did, and the gates began to swing open. 'How was I supposed to know that?'

'That's why I'm here. Let's get inside quickly.'

They took the two-minute walk to the house, and Rose noticed there was not a front door knob. 'Hold your watch over the door jamb.'

Rose nodded and the door swung open. *'Welcome home. I'm IVY, and I hope you enjoy your stay.'* Rose stepped inside, and the man followed her. The décor was very modern, simple, and elegant, much like she expected from another property owned by Nic. Uncle G-P pulled out a kitchen stool and sat down. 'What do you think of it?' Rose was about to respond but had more urgent things to deal with. 'Sorry, where is the bathroom?'

'The second door on the left, down the passage.'

Rose found the bathroom, and it was styled, be-fitting Nic's taste. Whilst she was wiping her hands, noticed one of the bathroom cupboard doors was not properly closed and her inquisitive nature got the best of her. Rose felt an urge to open the door to get a peek into the domain of Nic Thorns 'manly' stuff, but it was full of shampoos and moisturisers.

Rose quickly closed the door and returned to the lounge area. Uncle G-P turned on the television and it was tuned to the six o'clock news. He nodded at Rose. 'There's about to be a press conference from the Aged Care Minister'

'OK, but can I ask you a couple of questions?'

'Sure.'

'Whose place is this?'

'Nic's....oh sorry, Nicole's. It's Nic's sister's place. Didn't he mention that? Nicole works away, so the place has been empty for several weeks. It's for sale, so there's no one living here. I've been looking after it.'

Rose nodded. 'But surely they, whoever they are, have resources to know I could be staying here?'

'Possibly, but we'll worry about that later. Next question?'

'How long have you known Nic?'

'About thirty years.'

Rose nodded. 'Hang on, he calls you Uncle Grumpy-Pants, and he's in his mid-thirties. You must have known him longer than that.'

'You'll have to ask Nic about that. Besides, the news is starting.' Uncle G-P ignored the question and turned up the volume. The Aged Care fraud was the main story, but it began with a news cross to a reporter standing in front of the Queensland State Parliament building. The Opposition Leader was calling for a Royal Commission into the Aged Care portfolio, and while the story was concise, the reporter didn't have many other details.

It was then suddenly interrupted as the news-reader had a news alert: *'Sorry, we've had to cut that story short; we have just learned that they will be looking for a new State of Origin Coach. Wayne has refused to take the role.'*

Rose looked at the television and smiled. 'Only in Queensland does a rugby game take priority over everything else. Do you know what the fraud thing is all about?' Uncle G-P nodded. 'Sort of, the sinister minister has been actively adding to a slush fund. It's been going on for about four and a half years.

'Which one? Paul Roberts or Phillip Robertson?'

'The Robertson chap is the culprit. The Aged Care Minister, The Honourable Mr Paul Roberts, denies all knowledge. He's using the old 'three monkeys' defence. 'I see nothing, I hear nothing, and I say nothing'. What an ape.'

Rose was about to ask another question when her phone rang. Uncle G-P noticed. 'Gee, you're a Nervous-Nellie, aren't you? And yet you still work with Nic.'

Rose nodded. 'I wasn't like this before I met him. I'm just a bit tired.' Rose looked at the caller's name; it was Nic.

'Hi, Nic. What's up? I'm here with your Uncle Grumpy-Pants. Are you making a house call too?'

'No, I'm just letting you know that you can come home to Brisbane. The story has been bumped from the headlines. The Parliament is not sitting now, so it will be at least a few days before everything is revealed in question time.'

About two hours later, Rose had been dropped off at West End, and they were all sitting on the back deck. Nic took a sip of his chai tea, patted Dog, who had found his way onto his lap and looked over at Rose. 'Hey, I've got some bad and good news.'

'Ok, hit me with it.'

'Well, we have to go and watch question time in Parliament on Friday. We'll sit in the gallery when the brown stuff hits the spinning thing.'

Rose looked at him. 'Was that the good news or the bad news?'

'You choose.'

Nic continued. 'The Aged Care Minister, Mr Roberts, was sent an anonymous email. It showed that 'GOT Rubbish?' was owned by none other than Phillip Robertson, and that's where it all started.'

Rose nodded. 'OK, but I don't get it.'

'Chewy did some more investigations, and it turned out the Aged Care guy had been dodging up the invoice amounts on the rubbish collection service, and signing off the approval for the payment of the invoices.'

'So?'

'Well, once he got away with the small stuff, he started invoicing up for house construction, then commercial building renovations and even purchased a couple of yachts. Chewy found them all registered in his name. He'd been getting away with it for years.'

'That's crazy.'

'Yep. So, Chewy put it together and sent the anonymous email.'

Rose grinned. 'And then it collapsed pretty quickly? I supposed some jail time would be expected?'

'Well, it depends on what happens on Friday during question time.'

26

On Friday, Nic's group were sitting in the gallery, waiting for the axe to come down during question time. It didn't take long before the name-calling and yelling started up, and Nic looked down at the fracas, then leaned back to his group. 'That's weird, as it appears our little scamming guy is not here. He must have gone for a coffee and a cigarette to miss all the fun. We might need to leave.'

Rose whispered. 'Do we have to go? I like listening to how our taxes are spent.'

Nic nodded. 'I'm afraid so, but only to the high-set gazebo in the middle of the Botanic Gardens next door. I bet he's sitting there contemplating how he's going pay back all the money.'

Sandy leaned forward. 'How do you know he will be there?'

Nic grinned. 'He's a creature of habit, along with scamming the taxpayers he smokes O.P's and as it's after three, school is out.' They quietly moved to the rear stairs, out from the building and headed down the main path.

Rose stopped. 'What's with O.P.s?'

Nic smiled. 'Other Peoples cigarettes. He'll be bumming free ones from the kids. Anyway, this might get interesting, so be ready for anything.'

'Do you know what he looks like?

Nic nodded. 'Yep, he's the guy on the steps playing with a Zippo lighter. '

The man shook the lighter a few times and finally, it ignited, but he didn't have anything to smoke. A flock of schoolkids passed, and the man stood up to ask for a cigarette. One was handed over, and after a few attempts, lit the cigarette, took a long draw and sat down.

Nic held out his arm to stop Rose and Sandy from getting any closer. Rose noticed he had a solid silver beam across his back. 'What's he's carrying on his back?'

'A scooter. It folds up and he carries it over his shoulder. It's the chosen mode of transport of all low-level government employees.'

Rose nodded. 'So we might have to run after him if he takes off. Those things can get quite a speed up.'

'It's a 'boot-scooter', not an electric one. All we need to do is wait and watch, besides that, it's mainly uphill around here.' Nic directed the group to sit on a park bench and a couple of suited gentlemen headed towards Phillip.

Nic nodded toward them. 'Oh, that's not good. It looks like the brown stuff has already appeared in front of the fan. These two guys are the Detectives from the Fraud Squad.'

'How do you know?'

Nic nodded. 'Our man has just noticed them too, and he looks like he's on the move. The man stood and rolled the boot scooter from his back.

Nic then stated aloud. 'Not unless he goes underneath the gazebo to access the green-keepers area. It's where they store the lawnmowers, and there's petrol there, too. He might be planning on doing something stupid now that the noose is closing in on him.'

The man waved at the oncoming Officers, hopped onto the scooter, and headed toward the storage area. They watched as he kicked the door open and he momentarily disappeared from prying eyes. There was the sound of empty cans being strewn about as crashing and clanging from the storeroom.

After a few minutes, the man emerged with a can marked "Danger Petrol" and waved it at the two Detectives. 'Don't come any closer, you two. I've got the can and nothing to lose.'

Nic jumped up. 'Yep, he's doing something stupid.' Nic looked at Rose and Sandy and ran toward the developing situation. 'Stay here, guys, as it might get nasty and flamey.'

The two Detectives began to cordon off the area, and Nic stopped wandering walkers from coming further. They gathered the orange plastic safety cones and rope from a pile nearby and formed a large circle around the man. Phillip called out. 'I mean it. Step back, everyone. Don't try anything.'

The younger of the Detective's responded. 'It's not the way to end things, Mr Robertson. Think of your family.'

'I am. Now, move out of the way. Let me through.'

Nic responded. 'You know we can't do that, Phillip.'

'Who are you?'

'I'm the man that is here to stop you from getting fired.'

'Did you say fired or fried?'

'Your choice, Phillip. Put the petrol can down, and let us talk about this.'

Meanwhile, Sandy and Rose had gathered more rope and safety cones together and placed them across other paths to prevent access to the main Concourse area. It looked like a giant chess game using witches' hats. Rose looked over to Sandy. 'Don't you think it's very convenient that all these safety cones and ropes are around?' Sandy shrugged then they moved toward the main access gates at Albert Street and closed them off too.

Small crowds were collected at each closed path, and some started filming the event on their phones. Local TV crews were beginning to arrive. Phillip put his hand in his pocket and pulled out his Zippo lighter. 'It's not going to take much to set this stuff alight. Get back, get me a car so I can get away.'

Nic responded again. 'That's not going to happen, Phillip. Let's talk this through.'

The man looked around and appeared to be calculating his next move when one of the Detectives approached Nic and this meant only the second Detective was guarding the other exit toward the main entrance. Phillip must have realised this was an opportunity to make his move, so he slowly headed closer to the exit.

Rose noticed that Nic and the other Detective hadn't moved and wondered what was going on. It was a stalemate.

Phillip had gained some ground and carefully stepped over the rope cordon, but this meant he was closer to the water-lilied lagoons and birdlife. Rose and Sandy stepped back from their position. 'This doesn't make sense, Sandy, but I suspect Nic is up to something.' Nic feigned a move, and Phillip stepped backwards onto a wooden observation platform by the lagoon.

Phillip called out. 'Don't come any further. I mean it. I've got nothing left.'

Nic took a step closer. 'You haven't spent all the money, Phillip. It's sitting in your Bank account. You can sell the yacht, the cars and your shares. The house you bought at Bulimba has probably doubled in value. Please don't do anything stupid.'

'That's what they told me at Uni. Don't do anything stupid. I'm not stupid.' He then proceeded to tip the contents of the petrol can over his head. The liquid sloshed down his clothes and pooled at his feet.

The crowd all stepped back, and some of them started screaming when suddenly, a cry of 'enough' split the silence, and a young man vaulted over the rope and ran towards Phillip who was desperately trying to ignite his lighter. It finally caught, and the flame began to flicker, but the fluid did not ignite. The man tackled him mid-thigh and they both toppled into the water.

Some of the liquid had spilled onto the young man's suit and he stood up in the knee-high water trying to brush it off. 'Please don't light up. This stuff is flammable...' He stopped mid-sentence and took a big sniff of his forearm. 'This stuff smells like Listerine.'

Nic stepped into the pond. 'Yep, it is. And Phillip, can you hand me the can, please?' Phillip looked at him, lifted the can from the pond, and poured some of the remnants onto his hand. 'It's not petrol at all.' The lead Detectives beckoned Phillip to step out of the pond and then led him to a waiting Police van.

The young man had remained in the water, and Nic waded over to him. 'It looks like you've spoilt your suit. Was it new?' He nodded. 'Yes, and now I'm late for a job interview in Riparian Plaza.'

Nic smiled, then made a phone call. 'I've arranged a new suit for you at Clay Rotondo. It's just next to The Stamford and I've let them know you're on the way. Don't worry about the interview. I think the TV channels caught most of it and will support any excuse for why you are late. Please let me know how it goes. What was the job interview for?'

The man didn't instantly respond as they climbed out of the pond, so Nic added. 'It wasn't petrol, and you were right, it was Listerine.'

They shook hands and Nic added. 'That was courageous of you to tackle the guy and take him down.'

The man shrugged. 'I was late, and he was annoying me, and sometimes you just have to do something before someone else does. The job interview is with the Australian Security Intelligence Organisation, ASIO. Have you heard of it?'

Rose and Sandy moved toward Nic, and they watched the man hurry away.

A few days later, they were at Sandy's place, and Nic was going over the take-down. 'Sometimes scammers are so predictable. He took the only one that had anything in it, without checking it was petrol.'

Rose looked at him. 'I guess all the others were empty?'

Nic nodded. 'Yep, and thanks for quickly setting up the ropes and safety cones.'

Rose added. 'What about the young man that tackled him? Was he one of yours?'

'Nope, he was just walking through the gardens, minding his own business on his way to a job interview. Sometimes, you don't have to wear a superhero suit to be a real hero.'

Sandy nodded. 'Did you find out who he was? We didn't get a good look at him, and we could use a good-looking young guy in Nic Thorn and Associates.'

Nic laughed, stood up and started descending the stairs. 'Sorry guys, places to be, faces to see, and more scams to solve.'

Rose called out. 'Ok, but can I ask you one question before you go?'

'Sure.'

'Who is Uncle Grumpy Pants to you? And what's his real name?'

'Sorry, Rose, I'm getting hard of hearing these days. I'm nearly forty, you know. Besides, I think that was two questions.' Nic had moved further away so Rose leaned over the balcony and Nic stopped to look back.

'I've got a question for you, Rose. How is your arm? I heard that a woman barged into you at the Gallery in Sydney.'

Rose called back. 'How did you know? Oh, that's right, find stuff, lose stuff and know stuff, but why is that stuff a big deal?'

'Did you get a good look at her?'

'Not really, why?'

'That was Nicole, my sister. Chewy told me she would be at the gallery about the same time as you guys, so I tried to get her to stop, but she didn't take the call. She's OK, though, thanks for asking.'

Rose sighed. 'Can I ask you another question?'

Nic looked at his watch. 'Is it about Uncle Grumpy-Pants?'

'No. It's about the 'EAR' on the emails, and lots of P & S?''

'EAR....that meant "Eat After Reading..... with lots of Pepper and Salt."

Rose called out. 'You dope.'

'So, did you guys destroy the notes?'

Rose nodded. 'We burnt them... By the way, the correct ACRONYM is "BAR–*Burn* After Reading." Everyone knows that from the secret spy manuals.'

Nic nodded. 'OK then my super-league spy sleuths, how do you guys feel about getting smashed?'

Rose looked over to Sandy before replying. 'You know we don't drink that much, Nic.'

'I'm not talking about using alcohol, I'm talking about using a car.'

Nic moved towards his car, stopped, and called back.

'Can I assume from your non-response, guys, that it's a yes?'

Dedication

So, Rose, my fair lady, people don't bother me, for there's nowhere else on earth I would rather be than busting scams with you. Sure Nic, and I've grown accustomed to your face.

Keep reading an excerpt from the next adventures of Nic Thorn and Associates: 'Six Geezers Lying.'

It was a warm, sunlit morning at the Adelaide International Raceway in the outer northern suburb of Virginia, South Australia. Rosemary Palmer was surrounded by the sweet symphonic sounds of highly tuned engines. Puffs of blue and grey smoke swirled slowly through the throng of other car enthusiasts, but Rose was only here in Adelaide to assist with another scam investigation.

Meantime, her BFF Sandy Fraser was leaning into the engine bay of a 1976 Ford Falcon coupe, the bonnet was raised, and she was watching a Course Marshal tinker with a cable in the engine.

Their friend and business partner, Nic Thorn, was sitting in the driver's seat, and his foot was poised over the accelerator, waiting for the marshal to complete his inspection. He smiled and called out above the din. 'I love the smell of nitromethane in the morning.'

The uniformed official stood up, nodded, gave the thumbs up and moved away. Nic pressed his foot down, and the engine roared, much to Sandy's annoyance, so she signalled him to cut the engine, closed the bonnet and looked at him. 'What was that all about? He didn't do much apart from putting some gaffer tape over a toggle thing attached to a cable.'

Nic stepped out of the car. 'Ah, the secrets of motorsport. These races are timed events, so they switch off the line to the speedometer, and the drivers have to go around the course without knowing what speed they are going as the Marshal tapes the toggle in the off position so it can't be tampered with.'

Their group looked around at the other cars undertaking the same modification in their engine bays, and Rose nodded, 'I hope he knows the engine in is the back of those two VW Beetles over there?'

'I'm sure he does.' Rose continued. 'You know, if they turn off the cable to the transmission, it prevents the mandrel from spinning, and the magnets don't rotate in the speed cup. It makes sense.'

Nic looked at her. 'Wow, I didn't realise you were a petrolhead.'

'Yep, and there's so much about me you don't know.'

Rose glanced over to Sandy. 'Did you find anything interesting under the hood?'

'Nope, just a few nuts and bolts and an engine. It's always the nut sitting behind the steering wheel that we're all terrified of.'

For more reading from Nic Thorn and his associates of scam-busting capers:

One Tricked Phony

Rose needed a +1, but not for the usual wedding/party as she was going to a funeral and needed a quiet, unassuming type but when Nic Thorn arrived he coerced Rose and her BFF, Sandy into a series of madcap investigations of scams, frauds, and misunderstandings. These adventures involve a portrait provenance, invoice inaccuracy, and a recycler's relapse, on their travels from Brisbane, Adelaide, to the SA border.

Two hurtled Gloves

Welcome back to Nic's world of diversions and distractions, which begins on a golden beach in Port Douglas, tracks down to Tasmania, and up to the banks of Brisbane. Nic has to investigate a wedded miss, the misguided pretence of Tiger tracking, and then back to Brisbane to handle some banking bastardry.

Three French Bens

Nic's friend, Benoit Trudeau, is one-third of the 'Three French Bens'. He has just bought into a high-end restaurant in Melbourne, so he calls Nic to have a look, as the numbers look fishy. Then Nic and his crew head to Rockhampton to help the Queensland Department of Ag look into some cattle duffing, and finally, Sandy has to deal with an old school friend, who has been banking on bending the truth.

Four brooding Birds

Nic and the team head to Western Australia to investigate reptile smuggling, then the team must stop a scammer from drinking sweet success of wine in Margaret River. Finally, they must look into genuine budgie smugglers west of Broken Hill.

Six Geezers Lying

This time the team are back in Adelaide as car insurance companies are driven up the wall by bogus claims and 'accidents' Then a national restaurant chain runs a competition where the winners are drawn before the competition is closed, and finally back in Brisbane, Rose believes her Father is in the middle of an art scam. Art is not always art, but fraud is always a fraud.

Seven hapless Hoops

Organisations continue to look to Nic Thorn and his Associates to sort their stuff out. The wife of Nic's friend goes AWOL and it's a little close to home for Nic to ignore. Then a car vanishes without a trace in Mildura, someone keeps digging up the past in Canberra, and a bogus horse race is gathering pace on Kangaroo Island.

The author is a former long-term banker by profession and worked within the Bank's Credit Card Fraud Team, where he obtained a Private Investigators Licence. The author resides between Adelaide, South Australia, and the Sunshine Coast, Queensland.

In November 2022, the author won an award from Wakefield Press, Adelaide for his short story: 'Car on a Hill'.